Henry Duff Traill

William the Third

Henry Duff Traill

William the Third

ISBN/EAN: 9783337423728

Printed in Europe, USA, Canada, Australia, Japan

Cover: Foto ©Andreas Hilbeck / pixelio.de

More available books at **www.hansebooks.com**

WILLIAM THE THIRD

BY

H. D. TRAILL

London

MACMILLAN AND CO.

AND NEW YORK

1892

First Edition, May 1838
Reprinted, August 1888, 1892

CONTENTS

CHAPTER I

1650–1672

CHAPTER II

1672–1678

CHAPTER III

1678–1688

CHAPTER IV

1688

CHAPTER V

1688–1689

CHAPTER VI

1689

CHAPTER VII

1689–1690

CHAPTER VIII

1690-1691

CHAPTER IX

1691-1692

CHAPTER X

1692-1693

CHAPTER XI

1693-1694

CHAPTER XII

1695-1697

CHAPTER XIII

1698-1699

CHAPTER XIV

1699-1700

CHAPTER XV

1701-1702

CHAPTER I

Birth, ancestry, and early years—State of Dutch parties—William's
boyhood—His character and ambitions—Hostility of De Witt
and his partisans—Visit to England—Outbreak of the War of
1672.

WILLIAM HENRY, Prince of Orange and Count of Nassau,
a ruler destined to play a greater part in shaping the
destinies of modern England than any of her native
sovereigns, was born at the Hague on the 4th of
November 1650. By blood and ancestral tradition
he was well fitted for the work to which he was to
be called. The descendant of a line of statesmen and
warriors, the scion of a house which more than a century
before had been associated with the most heroic struggle
for national freedom that history records, he could hardly
have added stronger hereditary to the great personal
qualifications for the enterprises reserved for him. His
family was one of the most ancient in Europe—reaching
back, indeed, for its origin into the regions of fable. "I
will not take upon me," says an English biographer,
writing shortly after his hero's death, "to extend the
Antiquity of the House of Nassau as far as the time of

Julius Cæsar, though that Emperor in his first book of Commentaries, *De Bello Gallico*, says that one Nassua, with his brother Cimberius, led a body of Germans out of Suabia and settled upon the banks of the Rhine near Treves, which is the more observable by reason of the Affinity of the Words, which differ only in the Transposition of one Letter; but I doubt 'tis rather Presumption than Truth for any one to affirm that there is an Estate upon that very Spot of Ground mentioned by Cæsar which belongs to the Nassovian Family to this Day." Without insisting on so very ancient and remote an origin as this, we may take it as certain that the House of Nassau had been established in Europe for some thousand years at the birth of William. As early as in the thirteenth century it was honoured with the imperial dignity in the person of Adolph of Nassau. The title and domains of Orange were added to the family in the sixteenth century by the marriage of Claude de Chalons, sister and heiress of the then Prince of Orange, with Henry of Nassau, from whose son Réné the principality passed by testamentary bequest to the great Stadtholder of Holland, William, surnamed the Silent, the illustrious liberator of the United Provinces from the yoke of Spain. The acquisition of this petty principality—only twelve miles in length by nine in breadth—was by no means the matter of trivial importance which its territorial dimensions might imply. Its situation in the very heart of the dominions of France, the incidents attaching to that situation and the consequences flowing from it, contributed in their degree to that complex system of forces by which the course of history is determined. To William I. succeeded his son

Maurice, the bearer of a name also memorable in the history of the States, a greater soldier and a statesman of scarcely less ability than his father, though of a far more chequered fame. Under Maurice the power of the Stadtholder or Governor was, in spite of the jealousy with which it was regarded by the burgher party, considerably advanced, and he was not without reason suspected of the design of making himself an absolute ruler. Dying without issue, he was succeeded by his brother Frederick Henry, another renowned captain, under whom the long struggle with Spain was at last brought to a close by the renunciation, in the Treaty of Westphalia, of the Spanish claim upon the United Provinces. William II., the son of Frederick Henry, was born in 1626, and succeeded his father at the age of twenty-one. Endowed with all the restless activity and ambition of his uncle, he attempted, in prosecution of the same monarchical designs as that prince, to seize the city of Amsterdam by a *coup de main.* The project, however, was defeated, and William, after a troubled reign of only four years, was fatally attacked by the smallpox, and died on the 27th of October 1650, leaving no issue. Eight days after his death, however, his widow, Mary, daughter of Charles I., gave premature birth to the son whose career it is in these pages proposed to trace.

Seldom has a new-born child been the object of such diverse emotions, the centre of so many conflicting hopes and fears among its countrymen as was this infant Prince. To the partisans of the House of Orange he appeared as the God-sent heir—an earlier *enfant du miracle* vouchsafed by Providence to save the great race of William the Silent from extinction in the male line. To the party of the municipal oligarchy he presented himself as the probable inheritor rather of the ambitions of his father and his father's uncle, than of the virtues of his great-grandfather. The latter party, who for the moment had the upper hand, were fully resolved that the young Prince should never wield as much power as that which Prince Frederick Henry had sought during his four years' reign to abuse. The party of the infant Prince, on the other hand, a party headed by the Princess Dowager and her mother, made up as far as possible for the lack of direct and political power by incessant and indefatigable intrigue; and to their efforts it was that the Pensionary De Witt, the representative of the municipal party, ascribed, and not without reason, the war which broke out between the States and the Rump Parliament in 1651. Its effect, however, was temporarily disastrous to their ambitions; for, the United Provinces being compelled to solicit peace from Cromwell, the Lord Protector, who was naturally opposed to the elevation of a family allied by marriage to the exiled Stuarts, compelled the States of Holland and West Friesland, as a condition of his ratifying the articles of peace, to pass a decree that "they would never elect the Prince or any of his lineage Stadt-holder of their province, nor consent that he or any of his family should be Captain-General of the forces of the United Provinces."

Reared from his very cradle amid the animosities of contending factions, the young Prince learned early those four lessons of statecraft,—to conceal his designs, to watch his opportunities, to choose his instruments, and to bide his time. His education, other than that which he was receiving daily in the stern school of circumstances, he owed to his mother alone. Under her care he acquired a good knowledge of mathematics and military science, and learned to speak English, French, and German almost as fluently as his native tongue. The chiefs of the municipal party, who became his official guardians, would have willingly stinted his instruction, if by so doing they might have checked his aspirations; but the ambition to emulate the fame of his great predecessors, and to secure the power which they had wielded, took root within him from his boyish years, and grew steadily with his growth. Weak and ailing from his childhood, for he shared the too common lot of those infants who are brought into the world before the appointed months are run, he took no pleasure, as he possessed no skill, in the ordinary pastimes of the boy; and, with a mind thus turned inward upon itself, from an age at which other children have no care or thought but for the thousand novel interests and attractions of the world without them, he acquired habits of reserve and thoughtfulness beyond his years. The religious faith in which he was nurtured was a Calvinism of the strictest sort. His firm hold of the grim doctrine of predestination stood him in much the same stead as Napoleon's belief in his destiny, and long before he arrived at man's estate he had in all probability convinced himself that the inscrutable counsels of Providence had designed him for great things.

Humanly speaking, however, his prospects did not appear to brighten before him as years went on. At the age of ten he lost his mother, who had gone to England to visit her brother, just restored to the throne, and was there carried off by an attack of smallpox. In

.the same year he saw his principality of Orange forcibly seized by Louis, who, after demolishing its fortifications, held possession of it for five years, surrendering it only in 1665. Then came the war of that year between England and the Dutch Provinces, a conflict which his party temporarily conceived the hope of turning to their own profit, but which left them ultimately in a worse plight than before; for no provisions in the Prince's interests were insisted on by his uncle, Charles II., in the Treaty of Peace, and, under the instigation of De Witt, the States of Holland and West Friesland subsequently passed a perpetual edict suppressing the office of Stadtholder. A faint effort was made by Charles II. through Sir William Temple to vindicate the rights of his nephew, but the efforts of the ambassador were coldly received by the Pensionary, and the matter dropped. De Witt now pushed his hostility yet further, and the States resorted to the ignoble and ungrateful measure of calling upon the young Prince to quit the house at the Hague which, though technically the property of the States, had been for many years the official residence of his family. To the Pensionary, who was charged with the communication of this order, William replied by a spirited refusal, directing his visitor to inform the States that he would not quit the house unless removed by force; upon which his persecutors, apprehensive no doubt of the odium which such a step would excite among the common people, who were many of them well affected to his historic family, allowed their demand to lapse. William, now eighteen years of age, determined to make a counter-move on his own part, and presenting himself before the assembly of the States of the province of Zealand, he proposed to them to elect him first noble of that province, a dignity which they had been wont to confer upon his ancestors at his then age. The Zealanders complied readily with the request, though they did not proceed, as had been expected, to elect him to the higher office of Stadtholder of the province; and except by entitling him to a seat in the States General as representative of the nobility of Zealand, the minor honours procured him nothing but the increased jealousy and suspicions of the party of De Witt. Sir William Temple, then ambassador at the Hague, with whom the Prince came into contact at this time, characteristically reports of him in his Letters as a "young Man of more Parts than ordinary and of the better Sort; that is, not lying in that kind of Wit which is neither of use to one's self nor to anybody else, but in good plain Sense which showed Application if he had business that deserved it; and this with extreme good and agreeable Humour and Dispositions without any Vice; that he was asleep in bed always at Ten o'clock; loved Hunting as much as he hated Swearing, and preferred Cock-ale before any Wine." In the year 1670 he managed after some diplomatic difficulties to pay a visit to London, where he received the attentions of a civic banquet, and of an honorary degree at Oxford, and where too he acquired a very shrewd perception of the King's leanings towards the religion of Rome.

But his day was now fast approaching. At the close of the year 1671 was concluded the ever-infamous Treaty of Dover. Charles transformed himself, with more than the celerity of the nimblest modern rat, from the champion of the Protestant faith in Europe into the ally of its deadliest enemy. Sir William Temple was recalled from the Hague, and the Triple League between England, the States, and Sweden, which that skilful envoy had taken so much pains to cement, was broken up. Early in 1672 war was declared by England against the Dutch, and the armies of Louis, pouring into the United Provinces, became masters of all their chief strongholds "in as little time," to quote the vigorous comparison of one of William's biographers, " as travellers usually employ to view them." The Prince's opportunity had come.

CHAPTER II

William elected Stadtholder of Holland—Murder of the De Witts—
Campaign of 1672-3—Successes of the Prince—Declared here-
ditary Stadtholder—Progress of the French arms—Marriage with
Mary—Negotiations of Nimeguen—Conclusion of the Peace—
Battle of St. Denis.

LOUIS XIV., like other military malefactors before and
since, was himself the creator of the enemy by whom
his power was to be shaken to its foundations. His
invasion of the United Provinces, an enterprise commenced with that contempt of public right in which no
other potentate has ever equalled him, and prosecuted
with that barbarity in which only Oriental conquerors
have ever surpassed him, was the means of raising to
power the one European foe by whom he was destined
to be successfully withstood. The municipal party,
unduly absorbed in the task of safeguarding the liberties
of their country against the supposed ambitions of a
single fellow-countryman, had wholly neglected the
protection of its very existence against the known
ambitions of a foreign aggressor. Most of their veteran
troops had been disbanded; the greatest posts in their
armies were in the hands of unskilled civilians; cities
garrisoned with considerable forces of soldiery opened

their gates and surrendered without firing a gun.
Popular indignation rose high.   Upon William, always
a favourite among the commonalty, and the inheritor of
a name ennobled not only by civil wisdom but by
military exploits, all eyes were turned.   An insurrection
in his favour took place at Dort, and the magistrates of
that city, intimidated by the clamour of the people,
passed an ordinance repealing the perpetual edict, and
made him Stadtholder.   Other cities followed their
example, and the States-General of the provinces confirmed their decrees.   The two De Witts, John and his
brother Cornelius, now the objects of popular suspicion
and hatred, were assassinated in a street riot; and the
people, as if inspired with new courage by the restoration
of a Prince of Orange to a position from which princes of
that name had so often led them to victory, turned
fiercely upon their French invaders.   Five thousand of
Louis's troops were repulsed before Ardenburg by the
bravery of no more than two hundred burghers, assisted
by the women and children of the town, and one hundred
garrison soldiers.   The citizens of Groningen, aided by
the spirited students of its university, defended themselves with equal vigour and good fortune against the
warlike Bishop of Munster, at the head of 30,000 soldiers,
compelling him to raise the siege.   It was evident that
a Dutch conquest was going to be no mere military pro-
menade, as had first appeared to promise, and Louis
thought it advisable to negotiate.   To the chief of a
state so desperately be-sted as were the United Provinces
at that moment, the terms offered to William by the
French monarch,—no less than the sovereignty of his
country under the protection of England and France,—

might well have appeared tempting. William rejected them with scorn. He would never, he said, "betray the trust of his country that his ancestors had so long defended." Solicitations addressed to him in the same sense by England met with the same reply. To Buckingham, who had pressed them upon him, and warned him that "if he persisted in his present humour he must unavoidably see the final ruin of his cause," he made the Spartan answer that he "had one way still left not to see that ruin completed, which was to die in the last dyke."

The winter of 1672-3 had stopped the progress of the French for the time, but William was unwilling to allow it to arrest his own action. He laid siege to the town of Woerden, and, though forced by the Duke of Luxembourg to retréat from it, inflicted heavy losses upon the enemy. Then, having invested Tongres, captured Walcheren, and demolished Binch, he himself retired reluctantly into winter quarters. In the following spring he besieged and took Naerden, and later on in the year achieved a still more important triumph in the capture of Bonn, which had been put into the hands of France at the beginning of the war. New honours now began to be contemplated by his grateful countrymen for their stout defender. The Stadtholdership of Holland and West Friesland was not only confirmed to him for life, but was settled upon his heirs male ; and on the same day the like dignity was conferred on him by the States of Zealand—an example shortly afterwards followed by those of Utrecht. Nor were his successes without effect upon his enemies. Charles, with whose subjects the war had never been

popular, concluded a peace with him after these two
summers of fighting, and offered his mediation between
the powers still at war, an offer which was accepted by
France.   Four years, however, were to elapse, and
many souls of brave men to be sent to Hades, before
this mediation took effect in a concluded peace.   In the
summer of 1674 was fought the fiercest engagement of
the whole war—the bloody and indecisive battle of
Seneff, in which William was pitted against the renowned Prince of Condé.   The young Prince had too
much to gain in reputation not to be eager to provoke
a battle, and the old soldier too much to lose to be
willing to accept one if it could be avoided; but
William succeeded in his object.   Condé was at first
victorious in an encounter between a portion of the two
armies, but he imprudently brought on a general battle,
which, after raging furiously for a whole day, left both
parties to claim the victory—"the allies because they
were last upon the field, and the French on the strength
of the great number of prisoners and standards they had
carried off."   "But whoever had the honour," adds Sir
William Temple, "both had the loss."   It was on this
occasion that Condé paid his famous compliment to the
Prince by describing him as having acted like an old
general throughout the action in every respect save that
of having "exposed himself like a young recruit."

For yet another four years, as has been said, this
struggle continued to rage, and, as it raged, to store up
in his heart that exhaustless fund of resentment against
Louis which underwent hardly any depletion till the day
of his death.   Several times were attempts made to
detach William from his Spanish allies and to induce

him to conclude a separate peace, but he remained firm against all such solicitations of betrayal. In vain did Arlington, specially commissioned for that purpose, endeavour to tempt him to the desertion of his 'allies by the offer of an English matrimonial alliance. William simply replied that his fortunes were not in a condition for him to think of a wife. Louis, however, was extremely desirous of peace on any honourable terms, and William, to meet him half-way, put forward a counter-proposal of a marriage between the King of Spain and the eldest daughter of the Duke of Orleans, to whom France should give in dowry the late conquered places in Flanders. This ingenious proposal for reconciling the vindication of Spanish and Dutch interests on the Flemish frontier with the maintenance of French military honour, can scarcely have been made with any other purpose than that of putting France in the wrong. William knew probably that it would not square with Louis's existing hopes and pretensions, and that whether Charles pressed it upon his cousin or not, it was pretty certain that no more would be heard of it. For the present, moreover, he was under no pressure to make a peace at all. The United Provinces had recovered their confidence and hopefulness, and were full of admiration for and attachment to their young leader. He had been actually offered the sovereignty of Guelderland, and though his politic moderation induced him to refuse it, opinion among the other provinces was divided as to the propriety of his rejecting the offer. Nothing, however, could have more strikingly illustrated the commanding position which he had attained among his countrymen than

the complete paralysis which overcame them in 1675,
during the fortunately brief period of the Prince's
suffering from a dangerous attack of smallpox. From
this disease, so fatal to his race, he recovered with
apparent promptitude, but it is only too probable that
it left deep traces behind it on his congenitally feeble
frame.

After much dispute the scene of the peace negotiations had been fixed at Nimeguen, and the Congress
met there in the month of July 1676. But the diplo-
matists there were still to deliberate for two years while
armies were fighting; and if William could have prevented it, the peace would not have been made even as
soon as it was. The next two years, however, were on
the whole years of success for France and of defeat for
the allies ; and early in 1677 William, of his own accord,
revived a project to which, when previously broached to
him, he had refused to listen. The terms submitted to
him during the deliberations at Nimeguen were intolerable, and yet, though he obstinately refused to accept
them, town after town was falling before the French
arms, and his country was at last beginning to weary of
the struggle. If he must at last be forced to assent to
distasteful conditions, why not, as the price of his assent,
obtain for himself a matrimonial alliance which, besides
bringing him a step nearer to the English throne, would
immensely strengthen his position as a representative of
the Protestant cause in Europe. A year before he had
sounded Temple as to a proposal for the hand of his
cousin Mary, the Duke of York's eldest daughter ; and
had been encouraged by that ambassador to hope for
success in his suit. He now more formally pressed it,

selecting the moment with considerable astuteness.
Neither Charles nor James had any liking for the match,
but the King was in the midst of a struggle with his
Parliament; his subserviency to Louis was inflaming
popular resentment against him, and a marriage of his
niece to William, more especially if it could be made
the means of bringing about a peace, appeared to promise the only means of extricating himself from his
difficulties. Danby, his minister, moreover, was just at
that moment trembling for his head, and was prepared
to exert himself to the utmost to save it by the only
means available — the detachment of his master from
the French alliance. William was reluctantly invited
to England, and it is clear, in the whole history of the
affair, that he felt himself from the moment of his
arrival to be *dominus contractûs*. With respect to the
question whether the business of the marriage should be
arranged before that of the peace or *vice versâ*, William
insisted upon his own order of procedure, and procured
its adoption. Charles consented to the marriage, and
compelled the assent of his brother. The States-
General, communicated with by express, immediately
signified their approval; and William, who had fortunately found the person and manners of his cousin
highly attractive to him, was married hurriedly and
privately at eleven o'clock on the night of the 4th of
November 1677, the anniversary of his birth. The King
of England did his best to reconcile his brother of France
to a match, the news of which, our ambassador at the
French Court told Danby, he received "as he would
have done the loss of an army," by representing it
as an important step towards a peace; but William

returned home with his bride, pledged only to his uncle to accept a basis of peace which was to a large extent, if not entirely, of his own formulation, and far more liberal to the allies than anything which France had proposed. Louis, however, was to get his own way after all. The United Provinces were now heartily sick of the war, and were, moreover, not uninfluenced by a party hostile to William, who felt or feigned apprehension of his designs upon the liberties of the Republic. The States-General accepted the articles of France, and having by their constitution the absolute power of peace and war, they were able, on the 11th of August, to conclude a treaty over William's head. Three days after the Prince, unaware, officially at least, that the signatures had been actually affixed to the treaty, made a dash upon the army of Luxembourg, then besieging Mons, and after a desperate encounter secured one of the most brilliant successes of the war. The next morning, however, advices arrived from the Hague of the conclusion of the peace, and William had the mortification of feeling that the fruits of a victory which had opened a way for the allies into the country of their enemy were to remain ungathered.

CHAPTER III

1678–1688

An interval of repose—Revival of continental troubles—Death of
Charles II.—Expedition of Monmouth—Mission of Dykvelt—
James's growing unpopularity—Invitation to William—Attempted
intervention by France—William's declaration—He sets sail, and
is driven back by storm—Second expedition and landing.

FOR the next six or seven years the life of the Prince of
Orange was to be unmarked by any striking external
incidents. He was occupied with all his wonted patience
in the reparation of the mischiefs of the Treaty of
Nimeguen, and in the laborious construction of that
great European league by means of which he was afterwards destined to arrest the course of French aggression.
In this undertaking, and in watching and retaliating
upon the encroachments which Louis XIV., almost on
the morrow of the treaty, began making upon its provisions, William was sufficiently employed. In 1684
these encroachments became intolerable. Louis having
vainly demanded of the Spaniards certain towns in
Flanders, on the pretext of their being rightful de-
pendencies on places ceded to him by the Treaty of
Nimeguen, seized Strasburg and besieged Luxembourg
in physical enforcement of his claim. Spain declared
war, and William, though thwarted by the States

c

(mainly through the instrumentality of the city of Amsterdam, which was always ill-disposed towards him), and denied the levy of 16,000 men which he had asked for, took the field notwithstanding in support of his Spanish ally. The united forces, however, were too weak to effect much. Luxembourg speedily surrendered, and as the result a twenty years' truce, on terms not very favourable for William, was concluded with France.

During this period, as always, affairs in England no doubt demanded general vigilance; but it was not till 1685 that they showed signs of becoming critical. The death of Charles, and the known designs of Monmouth, placed William in a very delicate position. During Charles's life-time he had extended his protection to the exiled Duke, and had even insisted so punctiliously on proper respect being shown to him, that a difference had arisen between William and the English Court with reference to the Duke's receiving salutes from the English troops, and was actually unadjusted at Charles's death. Upon James's accession, however, either to clear himself of all suspicion of abetting a pretender to the throne, or, as some have asserted, to thwart the new king's design of having his nephew seized and sent a prisoner to England, William procured his departure from Dutch territory. Monmouth retired to Brussels, but at the instance of James, who wrote a letter to the Governor of the Spanish Netherlands charging him with high treason, he was ordered by that functionary to quit the King of Spain's dominions, and returned to Holland. Then followed his ill-fated enterprise, throughout the brief course of which William maintained an attitude of strict loyalty towards his father-in-law. He not only despatched the six English and Scotch regiments in the Dutch service to assist in suppressing the insurrection, but he offered, if James wished, to take command of the royal troops in person. The offer was declined, very likely from motives of suspicion by the King, but it is impossible to suggest any plausible reason for questioning its *bona fides*. The idle story that it was prompted by William's disgust at Monmouth's proclaiming himself king, in breach of a promise to raise William himself to the throne, bears absurdity on its face. The Princess stood next in succession to the throne as it was; and if the Prince had conceived a project of anticipating his wife's inheritance, he certainly would not have entrusted the execution of that project to the feeble hands and flighty brain of Monmouth.

But two years had scarcely passed before it really became necessary for him to look after the interests of her reversion. As early as the spring of 1687 it was beginning to be suspected by men of foresight, both in England and in Holland, that James II.'s position was precarious. No one, indeed, who was capable of forming a correct estimate of his character and capacities could find in them any guarantees of prolonged rule. He was as obstinate and insincere as his father, as selfish and unscrupulous as his brother, while he was destitute alike of the former's power of enlisting the devotion of individuals, and of the latter's easy popularity with the common people. It would be unjust to him not to admit that many of his gravest difficulties were prepared for him in his brother's time, if not by his brother's means; but it cannot be denied that he had made astonishing haste to convert these grave difficulties

into the most formidable dangers. In little more than
two years from his accession in February 1685, his
nephew found it expedient to send over an emissary to
England for the purpose of sounding English political
leaders, not as yet, indeed, with any definitely-formed
design of intervening by force in English affairs, but
rather probably that, in the event of the King rendering
himself "impossible," the people might know where to
look for a substitute, and might understand that the
heiress-presumptive and her consort were not only the
most natural, but, as a matter of fact, the most eligible
choice for the people to make in the circumstances.
Dykvelt, a judicious diplomatist, made the best use of
his time, and while continuing to give no just ground of
remonstrance to James, to whom he was of course
nominally accredited, he managed to bring back infor-
mation and assurances of much value from many English
politicians of eminence.

Meantime, and while James was still industriously
undermining his throne, his relations with his destined
successor were becoming more strained. A dispute
arose between them with reference to the six English
regiments lent to the States under treaty. The King
made a demand that these regiments should be officered
by Catholics—a claim put forward either with the object
of insuring their fidelity to him in case of future rupture
with Holland, or else merely to invite refusal and create
a pretext for insisting on their recall. At any rate the
refusal came, and on James's demanding the return of
the troops, the States refused this also, appealing to
the terms of the treaty as only authorising the King of
England to require restitution of these forces in the

event of his being actually engaged in warfare with a foreign foe. An acrimonious correspondence ensued between the two governments; but James failed to move the States from their firm attitude. Equally unsuccessful was he in an attempt to inveigle the Prince into an approval of that policy of pretended toleration by which he was seeking to further the interests of the Catholic at the expense of those of the Protestant religion in England. A Scots lawyer named Stuart, who had taken refuge in Holland from the religious persecution during the late reign, having made, or been bribed to make, his submission to the royal authority, was procured to open a correspondence with the Grand Pensionary Fagel, in which he pressed the latter to advise the Prince of Orange to support his uncle's policy, declaring that James would not repeal the penal laws unless the tests were repealed also. Fagel for some time returned no answer, but at last, finding the rumour in circulation that the Prince had associated himself with the King's measures, he wrote a reply, which had no doubt been drafted by William, to the refugee's request. In this remarkably politic document the Prince contrived to hold the balance equally between the English Protestants, with whom he was particularly anxious to stand well, and the Catholic continental sovereigns, whom in his struggle with France he could not afford to offend. While maintaining his former attitude with regard to the tests, William declared that he would gladly see all other grievances on the part of the English Catholics removed. He would have no man subjected to punishment for his opinions, but—and on this point he instanced the practice of the States-General themselves with respect to Roman Catholics—he was not prepared to remove all official disabilities founded on religious opinion. This letter was forwarded by Stuart to the King, and was by him considered in council. Burnet declares that all the lay papists of England who were not engaged in the intrigues of the priests earnestly pressed him to accept the Prince's terms as being what would render them safe and easy for the future; but the King as usual was obstinate, and no resolution was taken on the matter.

During most of the remainder of this year the King was filling up the measure of his political offences. From March till October the dispute with Magdalen College had raged, and the breach between James and the once devoted Church of England proportionately widened. But at the end of the year 1687 a momentous announcement was made to the Court. The Queen was pronounced to be pregnant, and in July of the following year she was delivered of a male child. That an infant brought into the world at so opportune a moment should have been loudly alleged to be supposititious by the inflamed political partisans of the time was naturally to be expected. A word or two more will be said on that point hereafter; it is here only necessary to remark that whether William shared the suspicions of his partisans or not his outward behaviour on the occasion was irreproachable. He congratulated his father-in-law on the auspicious event; and the infant prince was duly prayed for in his private chapel at the Hague, until the protest hereafter to be referred to was made against the ceremony by his English partisans. Meanwhile the events of the eventful year 1688 had been ripening fast to their destined issue. The end of April had witnessed the second promulgation of the Declaration of Indulgence, and the ferment occasioned by that new assertion of the dispensing power. In July, in almost exact coincidence of time with the Queen's accouchement, came the memorable trial of the Seven Bishops, which gave the first demonstration of the full force of that popular animosity which James's rule had provoked. Some months before,[1] however, Edward Russell, nephew of the Earl of Bedford and cousin of Algernon Sidney's fellow-victim, had sought the Hague with proposals to William to make an armed descent upon England, as vindication of English liberties and the Protestant religion.[2] William had cautiously required a signed invitation from at least a few representative statesmen before committing himself to such an enterprise, and on the day of the acquittal of the Seven Bishops a paper, signed in cipher by Lords Shrewsbury, Devonshire, Danby, and Lumley, by Compton, Bishop of Northampton, by Edward Russell, and by Henry Sidney,

---

[1] In April or May. Macaulay (after Burnet) says May; and the point is of some importance, because if, as Ralph maintains and proves by reference to the date of the Elector of Brandenburg's death (an event referred to by Burnet as still prospective at the date of the conference with Russell), this interview really took place in April, it does prove, as Ralph says, that "measures were forming in England against the King and embraced in Holland before the second Declaration of Indulgence was published, or the Order in Council which was founded thereon, or the Prosecution of the Bishops was thought of; which his lordship (Burnet) holds of such weight for the justification of those measures." Ralph i. 998.

[2] One of Russell's arguments for immediate action was that James's soldiers, "though *bad Englishmen* and *worse Christians*, were as yet such *good Protestants* that neither were they attached to His Majesty, nor could His Majesty depend upon them." — Burnet *ap.* Ralph, *Hist.* i. 997.

brother of Algernon, was conveyed by Admiral Herbert to the Hague. William was now furnished with the required security for English assistance in the projected undertaking, but the task before him was still one of extreme difficulty. He had to allay the natural disquietudes of the Catholic supporters of his continental policy without alarming his Protestant friends in England; to win over the States-General, not by any means universally favourable either to his designs against James or to his attitude towards Louis (Amsterdam, for instance, had sided with the former monarch in his dispute with William about the return of the English regiments); and, above all, he had to make his naval and military preparations for a descent upon England without exciting suspicions, or provoking an anticipatory attack. That he managed matters with much address is evident from the result, but it is no less clear that luck was on his side. A quarrel of the French king with the Pope, on a question of diplomatic extra-territorial rights in the papal city, and his arrogant interference in the election of the Elector of Cologne, had arrayed against Louis the spiritual and temporal forces of Catholicism, represented respectively by the Papacy and the Empire; his ill-timed persecutions of Protestants, and certain prohibitive measures adopted by him against Dutch trade, had the effect of alienating his partisans in the States-General. In the meanwhile the combined blindness and obstinacy of James permitted William to prosecute his military preparations unmolested, if not unsuspected. These preparations were very extensive and conspicuous, and seem to have had their commencement at an earlier date than is consistent with Burnet's

theory referred to in the note on a previous page. It
was not, however, till the summer was beginning to
give place to autumn that they began to excite any
very distinct suspicions as to their object. The Cologne
quarrel formed a plausible excuse enough for them; for
if Louis, as events seemed to threaten, were to occupy
the Rhine provinces with an army, it would be obviously
necessary for Holland to stand on guard. By the middle
of August the French king had become uneasy, and
despatched a special envoy in the person of M. Bonrepos
to awaken James to a sense of his danger. He had
authority, according to Burnet (whom, however, Macaulay,
who mostly follows him, on this point contradicts[1]), to
offer James not only naval but military assistance to
repel the invasion with which he believed him to be
threatened. Bonrepos was directed by his master to
promise the King of England that ten or fifteen thousand
(others, according to Ralph, say thirty thousand) men
should be landed at Portsmouth if required, and asked
that that place should be put into his hands to keep the
communication between the two kingdoms. Sunderland,
acting perhaps *bonâ fide*, but more probably not, most
earnestly counselled James to reject the offer, and it was
rejected accordingly, the King's characteristic imbecility
of judgment being never more characteristically shown
than in his unwillingness to offend the patriotic prejudices of his subjects by accepting an offer which, had

---

[1] It is difficult to see why. Sunderland, in his *Apology*, distinctly
says, "I opposed to death the acceptance of them (the ships) as
well as any assistance of men, and I can most truly say that I was the
principal means of hindering both." Sunderland, no doubt, was not
the most veracious of men; but one does not see his precise motive
for lying on this matter.

he been aware of their true feelings towards him, he would have recognised as his last chance of saving his crown and kingdom. At this juncture Ronquillo, the Spanish ambassador, went out of his way to assure James of what he probably knew to be false, and certainly had no reason to believe true—namely, that no descent upon England was in contemplation on the part of William. On an early day in September, however, Albeville was despatched to the Hague with instructions to present a memorandum of complaint on the subject of the Dutch preparations; and the day following d'Avaux delivered, on the part of Louis, a threatening note to the States, in which he warned them to desist from their designs upon a monarch to whom he was bound by "such ties of friendship and alliance" as would oblige him, if James were attacked, to come to his assistance. That Louis's motive in taking this step was to commit his brother of England to the alliance which he pretended to exist it is almost impossible to doubt; but James, more and more bent upon repudiating the assistance of France the more necessary it became to him, did his utmost to assure the States that there was nothing in the nature of an alliance between himself and Louis. William, however, and his partisans in the States-General, asked nothing better than this excuse for continuing their preparations, and the Dutch armament was actively pushed forward. In October the final alienation of the Dutch friends of France was brought about by Louis's despatching an army under the Dauphin to besiege Philipsburg, and simultaneously issuing manifestos against the Emperor and the Pope. Avignon had been seized by him the day before the siege of Philipsburg was opened; and the attack on the latter place was followed by the rapid seizure of most of the important towns of the Palatinate.

On the 10th of October, matters now being ripe for such a step, William, in conjunction with some of his English advisers, put forth his famous declaration. Starting with a preamble to the effect that the observance of laws is necessary to the happiness of states, the instrument proceeds to enumerate fifteen particulars in which the laws of England had been set at naught. The most important of these were—(1) the exercise of the dispensing power; (2) the corruption, coercion, and packing of the judicial bench; (3) the violation of the test laws by the appointment of papists to offices (particularly judicial and military offices, and the administration of Ireland), and generally the arbitrary and illegal measures resorted to by James for the propagation of the Catholic religion; (4) the establishment and action of the Court of High Commission; (5) the infringement of some municipal charters, and the procuring of the surrender of others; (6) interference with elections by turning out of all employment such as refused to vote as they were required; and (7) the grave suspicion which had arisen that the Prince of Wales was not born of the Queen, which as yet nothing had been done to remove. Having set forth these grievances, the Prince's manifesto went on to recite the close interest which he and his consort had in this matter as next in succession to the crown, and the earnest solicitations which had been made to him by many lords spiritual and temporal, and other English subjects of all ranks, to interpose, and concluded by affirming in a very distinct and solemn manner that the sole object of the

expedition then preparing was to obtain the assembling
of a free and lawful Parliament, to which the Prince
pledged himself to refer all questions concerning the
due execution of the laws, and the maintenance of the
Protestant religion, and the conclusion of an agreement
between the Church of England and the Dissenters, as
also the inquiry into the birth of the "pretended Prince
of Wales"; and that this object being attained, the
Prince would, as soon as the state of the nation should
permit of it, send home his foreign forces.

About a week after, on the 16th of October, all things
being now in readiness, the Prince took solemn leave of the
States-General, thanked them for their past kindness to
him, called them to witness that the motives of his
enterprise were solely those set forth in his declaration,
namely, the vindication of the liberties of England, and
the defence of the Protestant religion, and commended
his wife to their care. The scene was an affecting one,
and many among the assembly were melted to tears;
only the Prince himself, says Burnet, "continued firm
in his usual gravity and phlegm." Two days later the
States came to a formal resolution to assist the Prince
of Orange with ships and forces on his expedition to England, having heard his explanations thereof and found
them satisfactory; and authorised their ministers at the
various European Courts to make use of this resolution
in whatever way they might find most convenient.

On the 19th William and his armament set sail from
Helvoetsluys, but was met on the following day by a
violent storm which forced him to put back on the 21st.[1]

---

[1] To make some capital out of the mischance the Haarlem and
Amsterdam Gazettes were ordered (Ralph declares) "to set forth a

On the 1st of November the fleet put to sea a second time, and for the first twelve hours held its course towards the north-west. It was calculated that thus the scouting vessels sent out by Dartmouth would carry back word that the landing might be expected to take place on the Yorkshire coast; and, this ruse successfully effected, the fleet tacked and sailed southward for the Channel. William was naturally most desirous to avoid a conflict with the English fleet, and the heavy weather which prevented Dartmouth from leaving the Thames enabled him to attain his object. His fleet passed the Straits of Dover at midday of the 3d of November, and made for Torbay, where it had been determined to land. In the haze, however, of the morning of the 5th of November the pilot overshot the mark, and took the fleet some miles to the west. Its situation became critical. Plymouth was the next port, and of Lord Bath, who there commanded the King's forces, William was by no means sure. From the east the royal fleet under Dartmouth was believed to be approaching. Russell, who had told Burnet that "all was over," and that he might "go to prayers," was just upon taking boat for the Prince's ship when the "Protestant wind," as the long prayed-for easterly gale had hitherto been called, having now by force of circumstances become a breeze of a distinctly Catholic tendency, was, as all good Protestants of that day believed, providentially lulled. A wind of the right direction and denomination sprang up shortly after, and in four hours' time, by noon of the 5th of November, the Prince's fleet was wafted safely into Torbay.

lamentable relation of the losses occasioned by it," losses which, it seems, included "nine men of war, a thousand horses, and Dr. Burnet."

CHAPTER IV

1688

THE spot was in one respect well, in another ill chosen for a descent. Nowhere, indeed, was James's tyranny more detested than in that quarter of England in which William now found himself, but nowhere also was it more feared. It was the country of the men who had risen for Monmouth and fought at Sedgemoor, but it was the country too of the men who had trembled before Jeffreys, and whose blood had given its name to his terrible Assize. The reception which William met with was in fact determined by a balance of these considerations. He was welcomed with abundance of popular sympathy, but with little overt popular support. The gentry and peasantry rejoiced at the sight of his standard, but were slow in gathering to it. His march to Exeter was something like a triumph, but it seemed at first, and indeed for some days after he had fixed his quarters there, that he was to get nothing from the people but their good wishes. That this delay

in supporting him gave much disappointment and even
some anxiety to William is certain. He was too politic
to make any public manifestation of feelings, the dis-
closure of which might only have served to aggravate
their cause; but in private he complained indignantly
of the slackness of his promised adherents, and even
talked—though here we may permit ourselves to doubt
his seriousness—of abandoning his enterprise and returning to Holland. At the end of a week, however, important partisans of his cause began to make their
appearance. Lord Colchester, a friend of Monmouth's,
was the first to join him; Edward Russell, a son of the
Earl of Bedford, followed; Lord Abingdon, a recruit
from the other side of politics, was the next to give his
adhesion to William; and almost at the same moment
the cause of James sustained the most significant re-
pudiation it had yet undergone in the desertion of Lord
Cornbury, the eldest son of Lord Clarendon, who, after an
unsuccessful attempt to bring over with him the three regiments of which he was the commander, deserted them with
a few followers and made his way to William's quarters.

   In London, ever since the news of the Prince's landing, considerable agitation had prevailed, and some
actual rioting taken place. But the royal authority
was still upheld, and it was evident that the action of
the capital, reversing the order of revolutionary proceedings to which France has now accustomed us, would
await the course of events in the provinces. As for
the King, he was, characteristically enough, as much
reassured by a week's respite from bad news as he had
been disturbed by the tidings of his nephew's landing;
but the intelligence of Cornbury's defection threw him

into a state of genuine alarm. Having convoked and
addressed the principal officers then in London, from
whom he received the most earnest professions of
loyalty, he prepared to set out to meet the invader at
Salisbury, when he was waited upon by a deputation of
the Lords, praying him to call a Parliament and to open
a negotiation with the Prince of Orange. James, however, to whom no measure ever presented itself as
advisable at the proper moment for adopting it, rejected their advice. His reason was an excellent one—
for any king in a totally different position from his.
He said, and with much truth, that no Parliament
could be freely chosen for a country with an invading
army encamped on its soil; but the question which a
clearer-sighted sovereign would have asked himself was
not whether the parliamentary elector would be a free
agent, but whether he himself was. It was eminently
probable that the convocation of a Parliament would not
save his throne, but it was quite certain that nothing
else would. Nor had James the excuse of pride for
rejecting the Peers' advice; he was to show in a very
short time that no such account of his conduct could be
sustained. Some monarchs might have preferred to lose
a crown rather than be forced into political concession
under coercion of an invading army. James was quite
willing to pay that or any other price to save his crown,
only he was impenetrable to the proof that it was necessary at that moment. He set out for his destined headquarters, and reached them on the 19th of November;
but by the time he established himself at Salisbury the
real royal court had collected itself at Exeter. William
was haranguing the "friends and fellow Protestants"

who had gathered to his banner, and continually receiving fresh adhesions, among which that of Lord Bath, the
commander of the royal forces at Plymouth, was the
most important. Meanwhile, the northern population
of the kingdom, among whom William had been expected
to present himself first, were up in arms. York and
Nottingham were the chief centres of insurrection, and
to one or the other of them many of the great peers
and landowners of the north were already making their
way. Placed thus between two fires, it was evident that
immediate action was necessary on James's part to prevent their meeting and engulfing him. As it was no less
evidently to William's interest to defer a conflict as long
as possible, he succeeded in avoiding anything save
mere skirmishes between outposts, until the occurrence
of an event for which he was probably prepared, and
which he had good reason to hope would insure the
triumph of his cause without any serious fighting at all.
This was no less an event than the desertion of Churchill,
who, if, as is likely enough, he had been up to this point
doubting to which side his interests pointed—the
only form of indecision he was liable to—had by this
time satisfied himself that James's cause was lost.
Alarmed by rumours of disaffection in his army, James's
eagerness for an encounter with William had now
entirely disappeared. He talked of retreating, but
Churchill strongly urged an advance. Whether, if his
counsels had prevailed, he would have taken over the
troops under his command to William, or whether he
would have awaited the issue of battle in order to obtain
still clearer light on the only question that interested
him, must for ever remain uncertain. James resolved to

fall back, and Churchill resolved not to accompany him. He quitted the royal camp that night, leaving behind him a letter, in which he declared it impossible for him to fight against the cause of the Protestant religion, and presented himself next day at the quarters of the Prince of Orange. His flight threw James into extreme consternation. A precipitate retreat was ordered, and the royal standard, now losing more and more followers every day, was soon being hurried back to London. Prince George of Denmark, who lives in history as *Est-il possible?* abandoned his father-in-law at Andover, and James returned to Whitehall to find that his younger daughter had followed her husband's example. "God help me!" the wretched King exclaimed; "my own children have forsaken me." A man so accustomed to subordinate all the kindlier instincts of human nature to the precepts of his religion might have recollected that Anne had only to identify the interests of Anglican Protestantism with the cause of Christ in order to find excellent Scriptural authority for turning her back upon her father.

It being now too late to hope for an accommodation with his people and their invited champion, James began to think of arranging one. He summoned a council of the Lords spiritual and temporal then in London, and signified his willingness to "agree with his adversary" slowly, and when no longer "in the way with him." He was ready now to take the advice which had been tendered him before he started for Salisbury—namely, to summon a Parliament and open negotiations with William. It was now, however, pointed out to him that, his position having become worse by delay, he must make an advance on his original offers by dismissing all Catholics from office, breaking off his relations with France, and promising an amnesty to all political opponents ; but as this or some similar enlargement of the original terms of concession submitted to him unmistakably recommended itself to common sense, the King would not hear of it. He would summon a Parliament, and at once did so by directing Jeffreys to issue writs convoking that body for the 13th of January. He would negotiate with William, and he named Nottingham, Halifax, and Godolphin as his commissioners for that purpose. But more than this he at first declined to do. On further reflection, however, it occurred to him that the pang of giving these distasteful pledges might be much mitigated by a secret resolve to break them. He therefore issued a proclamation granting a free pardon to all who were in rebellion against him, and declaring them eligible as members of the forthcoming Parliament. At the same time he gave an earnest of his willingness to conform to the law excluding papists from office by removing the Catholic Lieutenant of the Tower. Again, at the same time, and as the reverse of an "earnest" of anything, he informed the French Ambassador that the negotiation with William was "a mere feint," and that all he wanted was to gain time "to ship off his wife and the Prince of Wales." There was undoubtedly a good deal of his royal and unfortunate father about James II. He seems, indeed, to have inherited almost all Charles's moral qualities except his courage. These he "threw back" to his grandfather—not a fortunate illustration of the biological principle of atavism.

Infected with the duplicity and unredeemed by the bravery of Charles I., the close of his reign is naturally less romantic than his father's. Kings who fail in business undoubtedly owe it to their historical reputation to perish on the scaffold or the battle-field. A royal martyr is a much more impressive object than a royal levanter. It is better to "ascend to Heaven" as "the son of St. Louis" than to take ship for Dover as "Mr. Smith." The last three weeks of James's reign are weeks of painful ignominy. His plan of spiriting away the infant Prince of Wales was defeated by Dartmouth, the admiral on whom he had relied to execute it, but who steadfastly refused to lend a hand to the project. William's army advanced from Exeter to Salisbury, and from Salisbury to Hungerford, where it had been arranged that the royal commissioners should meet the Prince. The result of the negotiation was favourable beyond anything James had a right to expect. The Prince accepted his father-in-law's offer to refer all questions in dispute to the Parliament about to be assembled, stipulating only that the capital should be relieved from military pressure on either side; that James should, as a security against his inviting French aid, place Portsmouth under the command of an officer in whom both sides had confidence; and that, while London was denuded of troops, the Tower—as also Tilbury Fort—should be garrisoned by the city of London. It is by no means impossible that James might have saved a crown, however shorn of its prerogatives, had he accepted these terms. But he was bent on attempting to regain by foreign arms that full despotic authority which he could not retain by his own. He contrived, with the assistance of the chivalrous and eccentric Frenchman Lauzun, to get the Queen and Prince of Wales

conveyed safely to France ; and twenty-four hours afterwards, on the night of the 11th of December, he endeavoured to follow them, but he was recognised at the
Isle of Sheppey, whence he was about to embark, and
his flight arrested.   In London, where the royal forces
had, in obedience to James's parting orders, been disbanded by their commander-in-chief, some forty-eight
hours of very dangerous panic ensued upon the King's
departure ; but a provisional government was hastily
formed by a committee of temporal and spiritual peers,
and measures promptly taken by them for the maintenance of order.   On hearing of the capture of James, they
immediately despatched Feversham with a troop of Life
Guards to escort him back to London.   Here he was
received with some marks of popular commiseration,
which he mistook for reviving popular favour, and, re-
gaining confidence, he sent Feversham to Windsor as
the bearer of a letter to the Prince of Orange, express-
ing a desire for a personal conference with him at St.
James's Palace, which he offered to fit up for the Prince's
accommodation.   William, however, as one may now
see plainly, was bent on creating a vacancy of the
throne.   He no doubt keenly regretted the officiousness
of the sailors who had defeated James's first attempt at
flight, and resolved to do all in his power short of downright physical coercion to induce him to repeat the
attempt.   He arrested Feversham for want of a military
safe conduct, and replied to James's letter by declining
the conference, and desiring him to remain at Rochester.
The King had by this time reached Whitehall ; but,
disquieted by the sternness of William's message, and
by the arrest of his officer, his nerve began once more

to fail him. On the night of the 18th three or four
battalions of William's infantry and a squadron of horse
marched down to Whitehall, and, the English Guards
being withdrawn by the King's orders and to the
great regret of their stout old commander, Lord Craven,
took practical possession of the palace. In the small
hours of the morning Halifax and two other lords
arrived from Windsor with a recommendation to James
to retire to Ham. Ostensibly delivered in the name of
his own Peers, James felt satisfied that it was really a
hint from William. He proposed to substitute Rochester for Ham, and the substitution was accepted by
William with a readiness which significantly showed
his desire to facilitate his uncle's flight. Early the
next morning James, accompanied by Lords Aylesbury,
Lichfield, Arran, and Dumbarton—peers whose names
deserve if only as a matter of curiosity to be recorded,[1]
—set out for Rochester; and four days afterwards, with
motives which have been variously estimated, but in
which fear for his life or liberty and hopes of foreign
assistance towards the recovery of his kingdom played
perhaps about an equal part, he again resolved to quit
the kingdom. A letter from his Queen—intercepted
indeed, but which William took care to have conveyed
to him—confirmed his resolution. Between two and
three o'clock on the morning of the 23d he embarked
on board a frigate on the Medway, and, finding the wind
favourable, landed after a speedy voyage at Ambleteuse,
whence he proceeded to St. Germains.

[1] It is true that a large number of courtiers quitted Whitehall at the
same time, making the palace, as Ralph says, "like a Desart." But
the large majority of them got no further than St. James's.

CHAPTER V

1688-1689

Characteristics of the English Revolution—Views of the various parties
—The Convention — Proposal to declare the throne vacant—
The Regency question — The resolution of the Commons—
Amendment of the Lords—The crisis—Attitude of Mary—An-
nouncement of William — Resolution passed — Declaration of
Right—Tender of the crown.

IT is significant of the peaceful and, so to speak, constitutional character of our English Revolution that by
far its most momentous scenes were enacted within the
four walls of the meeting-places of deliberative assemblies, and find their chronicle in the dry record of votes
and resolutions. We have no "days," in the French
sense of the word, or hardly any, to commemorate.
The gradual accomplishment of the political work of
1688-89 is not marked and emphasised like that of
1789-92 at every stage by some out-door event of the
picturesque, the stirring, or the terrible kind—such for
instance as those by which the 14th of July, the 6th of
October, the 10th of August, and in a darker order of
memories, the 2d of September, have been made land-
marks in the revolutionary history of France. On
every one of the days thus singled out for glorious or for
shameful remembrance, some irrevocable step was taken
—some new position gained by the advancing forces of

French democracy from which there was no retreat. We in England have no anniversaries of the kind. We may remember, though we have ceased to celebrate in our churches, the day in which William first set foot on our shores; but we feel that after all it was not an "event" in the sense of that other great Protestant deliverance with which in month-date it so fortunately coincided, and for which the Anglican liturgy economically set apart a common form of thanksgiving. The discovery of the Gunpowder Plot was an incident having results of the most permanent and unalterable character. It made all the difference between the safety and the destruction of the Sovereign and the three Estates of the Realm. Again, the execution of Charles I. determined something, by committing the country to the military autocracy of Cromwell and the powerful reaction of the Restoration. But this cannot be said of the landing of the Prince of Orange at Torbay—the mere opening of a drama which might have had any one of half a dozen *dénoûments;* it can hardly even be said of the second and definitive flight of James. The 23d of December 1688 was in one sense no more of an "epoch-making" day than the 5th of November in the same year. It is true that the sovereign's abandonment of his throne and country became something more than a striking dramatic event; it was elevated into an act of profound political import. It had or was invested with inward and most momentous legal significance, in addition to its outward historical prominence. But for all that it determined nothing at the moment of its occurrence but the future of a single man. It is quite conceivable that the mere flight of James II. should have settled no more than his own incapacitation—that it should not even have brought about the exclusion of his son from the succession, still less have led to the formal recognition of a new principle. in the English Constitution. True it is that all these consequences were deducible from it as matter of argument, and flowed from it in fact. True it is that, when James stole down the Medway in the early morning of the 23d of December, he was taking a step which was capable of being turned by the friends of liberty and good government, or his own enemies,—and it was difficult to be one without being the other,—to the disherison of his son, and the far-reaching substitution of a statutory for a common-law monarchy. But no less true is it that these results were very far from being necessary or automatic in their character; that, on the contrary, they hung for some critical days in the balance, and that the active co-operation of human qualities in its very conspicuous and not too common forms of courage, foresight, and political dexterity, was needed in the last resort to secure them. It is for this reason that our "days," our anniversaries of such merely external incidents as William's landing or James's departure are, comparatively speaking, so unimportant. No such incident either made or insured the making of our existing English Constitution. The events which really made it passed, as I have said, within the walls of two deliberative assemblies, between January 23 and February 13, 1689, and its making was not actually assured until this period was well-nigh expired.

How important was the political work compressed

within these three weeks will be at once apparent if now, having noted how little was settled by the mere flight of James II., we go on to consider how great was the variety of its possible results. James had ceased to be king *de facto*, that was all ; and the English people were pretty unanimous in their determination that he should never be king *de facto* again. But was he still king *de jure* ? If not, if he was not legally sovereign, was any one ? And if so, who ? Upon each of these last three questions there was room for difference of opinion, and upon at least two of them opinion was in fact divided. A considerable section of the Tory party were of opinion that James, although he had *de facto* ceased to reign, was still the only lawful king of England, in whose name, at any rate, all royal authority should be exercised, and all royal acts of state performed. To these men, therefore, the only legal and constitutional solution of the problem appeared to be the creation of a Regency. They were for raising William to the position of Regent, and empowering him to preside over the actual government of the country in this capacity during the life of his father-in-law.

A second section of the Tory party held, on the other hand, that James having by his own act ceased to govern, had also ceased to reign. By deliberately laying aside the sceptre he had brought about a demise of the crown. It had simply devolved upon the person next in succession ; and that person was, they declared, the Princess Mary. There was no need therefore for the creation of a Regent, and still less for the more extreme and wholly unprecedented step of appointing a new sovereign. All that was necessary was a mere formal recognition by the country of the bare legal facts of the case. According to this party the Princess Mary was in truth at that moment the lawful Queen of England, and nothing more was needed than a national acknowledgment of her title.

To both of these doctrines the Whig party were equally opposed. They held in opposition to the former, that James had ceased to reign, and in opposition to the latter, that the crown had been not demised but simply forfeited. The King's destruction of his own right could not have, and had not had, the effect of transmitting them to any one else whomsoever. They resided at that moment, whatever constitutional fictions might aver to the contrary, in no one; and a special expression of the national will, a special exertion of the national power, would be required in favour of some designated successors to these rights before anybody could be regarded, whether in fact or law, as invested with them.

Apart from all political prepossessions there can, I think, be no serious dispute as to which was the most logical and tenable contention of the three ; and that this was distinctly that of the Whigs. The Tories who contended that James had lost his right to the personal exercise of the royal authority, while yet retaining so much of that authority that any one who exercised it in his stead must be supposed to do so as his deputy, were involved in a hopeless contradiction. In assuming to appoint such deputy to act for a person whom they still persisted in regarding as king *de jure*, they were themselves obviously usurping a portion of that very *jus* which they professed to respect. True, they attempted to get over this objection by urging that James had placed himself under a disability to exercise his royal authority, but they could point to nothing in the facts of the case to support their contention. Disability to exercise royal authority could, in the view of the Constitution, arise from one cause alone, the same cause from which in the view of the common law arises the disability to exercise civil rights. The disabled King, like the disabled subject, must have become mentally incapacitated; and James's incapacitation for the work of government was purely moral. Setting aside the deposition and execution of his father, which even the Whigs did not endeavour to elevate into a regular precedent, there was no constitutional sanction for the withdrawal of the reins of state from the hands of the monarch, on any ground save that of insanity. Once extend this, and admit that a king who is merely bad may be treated as though he were mad, and the Whig doctrine is thereby absolutely conceded. As to the practical inconveniences of a Regency exercised in the name of an actively hostile sovereign—a sovereign who would have been sometimes in arms against his own nominal authority, and always plotting its overthrow—they would of course have been both grave and numerous. But it is less surprising that the Regency party of that day should have ignored them than that they should have been so indifferent to the complete surrender of their political principles which was involved in the proposal to which they committed themselves.

More logical in form, but equally untenable in fact, was the position assumed by the other section of the Tory party. There was perhaps nothing altogether irreconcilable with their principles in the theory that a voluntary abandonment of the throne might operate as a demise of the crown; but coolly to assert a right to pass over the infant Prince of Wales on the strength of the mere idle story that he was a supposititious child[1] was a pretension which, especially as put forward by men who were such sticklers for constitutional fictions as to insist that there must at any given moment be some one person or other entitled to wear the English crown, appears little short of preposterous.

The Whig theory of the situation rejected the fictions of both branches of the Tory party with equal decision. There was no need, according to the Whigs, for the country to bewilder itself in efforts to distinguish between *de jure* and *de facto* sovereignty, still less to resort to the far-fetched expedient of assuming a demise of the crown in order to prevent the former kind of sovereignty from undergoing interruption. A king, they held, might lose his title to the crown by a voluntary abandonment of the throne; and he might lose that title without anybody succeeding to it. Indeed, since the English crown devolved according to the ordinary English laws of succession, it was impossible that anybody should succeed to it by mere *operation of law* during its former wearer's life-time. If it was a principle of constitutional law that at any given moment there must be some lawful king or queen of England in existence, it was no less a principle

---

[1] *How* idle this story was may best be judged by studying the so-called evidence in its favour, as set forth in the pages of that writer who, more perhaps than any other chronicler of the events of that period, would have liked to establish its truth. No one, I think, can read Burnet's account of the Queen's accouchement, so completely demonstrating as it does the *impossibility* of the alleged fraud, without wondering at the strength of the partisanship and popular prejudice which could for a moment have believed in its perpetration.

of the common law that *nemo est hæres viventis.* James, therefore, had according to the Whig theory ceased to be sovereign, and no one else had become sovereign in his stead : the throne was vacant. Being vacant it was for the Convention to fill it, and the members of that body were both entitled and bound to select the fittest successor to it, unconstrained, though not necessarily uninfluenced, by the claims of successorship which would have vested in this, that, or the other person under an ordinary demise of the crown.

That this was the most logical and self-consistent view of the situation appears to me undeniable ; but it is a singular illustration of the manner in which events may transpose the relative proportions of principles that this Whig corollary from the abdication of James appeared to the statesmen of the time, and even it should seem to Macaulay, a century and a half after them, to be a more pregnant assertion of democratic doctrine, and a bolder step in its application, than that expressed in the earlier proposition that James had ceased to reign. Nowadays the difference between the Tories who contended that the crown had been demised, and the Whigs who insisted that the throne was vacant, hardly arrests the student for an instant. He is disposed to brush the Tory fiction aside as alike irrational and unnecessary. The real passage of the Rubicon took place in his view of the matter when it was declared that James had ceased to be *de jure* king, and no subsequent assertion of popular rights in the choice of a successor could possibly be stronger or more important than that declaration itself. Yet whereas the Convention accepted the first of these propositions *nemine contradicente,*

the second was only adopted after having been once
actually rejected, and was in fact the subject of so sharp
a conflict of opinion as to threaten irreconcilable deadlock between the two branches of the constituent body.[1]

The Convention met on the 22d of January, when
Halifax was chosen president in the Lords; Powle,
Speaker of the Commons. A letter from William, read
in both Houses, informed their members that he had
endeavoured to the best of his power to discharge the
trust reposed in him, and that it now rested with the
Convention to lay the foundation of a firm security for
their religion, laws, and liberties. The Prince then went
on to refer to the dangerous condition of the Protestants
in Ireland and the present state of things abroad, which
obliged him to tell them that next to the danger of unreasonable divisions among themselves, nothing could be
so fatal as too great a delay in their consultations. And
he further intimated that as England was already bound
by treaty to help the Dutch in such exigencies as, deprived of the troops which he had brought over, and
threatened with war by Louis XIV., they might easily

---

[1] The fact that the *practical* cause of this sharp conflict was the
rivalry between the partisans of William and those of Mary is only a
partial explanation of the phenomenon referred to in the text. It is
a reason for the Convention having debated the Whig corollary so
much, but not for their debating the Whig-Tory original proposition
so little. Of course the *practical* explanation is the simple one, that
James had made himself impossible. Both parties concurred so
readily in that opinion that they applied it without either of them
pausing to consider its scope as a precedent, and that, quite apart from
all controversies as to regency, demise of the crown, vacancy of the
throne, or what not, the first instance in which a people pronounced
any king impossible—such king being of sound mind, and still assert-
ing his sovereignty—let in the whole modern democratic theory.

be reduced to, so he felt confident that the cheerful con-
currence of the Dutch in preserving this kingdom would
meet with all the returns of friendship from Protestants
and Englishmen whenever their own condition should
require assistance.   To this the two Houses replied with
an address thanking the Prince for his great care in the
administration of the affairs of the kingdom to this time,
and formally continuing to him the same commission,[1]
recommending to his particular care the present state
of Ireland.   William's answer to this address was characteristic both of his temperament and his preoccupation.
" My lords and gentlemen," he said, " I am glad that
what I have done hath pleased you ; and since you desire
me to continue the administration of affairs, I am willing
to accept it.   I must recommend to you the consideration
of affairs abroad which makes it fit for you to expedite
your business, not only for making a settlement at home
on a good foundation, but for the safety of Europe."   On
the 28th the Commons resolved themselves into a committee of the whole House, and Richard Hampden, son
of the great John, was voted into the chair.   The honour of having been the first to speak the word which
was on everybody's lips belongs to Gilbert Dolben, son
of a late Archbishop of York, who "made a long speech
tending to prove that the King's deserting his kingdom
without appointing any person to administer the government amounted in reason and judgment of law to a
demise."   Sir Robert Howard, one of the members for

---

[1] It is somewhat singular that Macaulay should have taken no
notice of an address which really constituted William's sole legal, or
quasi legal title to the administration of affairs between the assembling
of the Convention (which necessarily revoked his original commission)
and the conclusion of its king-making labours.

Castle Rising, went a step further, and asserted that the throne was vacant. The extreme Tories made a vain effort to procure an adjournment, but the combination against them of Whigs and their own moderates was too strong for them, and after a long and stormy debate the House resolved "That King James II., having endeavoured to subvert the constitution by breaking the original contract between the King and people, and by the advice of Jesuits and other wicked persons having violated the fundamental laws and withdrawn himself out of the kingdom, has abdicated the government, and that the throne is thereby vacant."

This resolution was at once sent up to the Lords. Before, however, they could proceed to consider it, another message arrived from the Commons to the effect that they had just voted it inconsistent with the safety and welfare of this Protestant nation to be governed by a Popish king. To this resolution the Peers assented with a readiness which showed in advance that James had no party in the Upper House, and that the utmost length to which the Tories in that body were prepared to go was to support the proposal of a Regency. The first resolution of the Commons was then put aside in order that this proposal might be discussed. It was Archbishop Sancroft's plan, who, however, did not make his appearance to advocate it, and in his absence it was supported by Rochester and Nottingham, while Halifax and Danby led the opposition to it. After a day's debate it was lost by the narrow majority of two, forty-nine peers declaring in its favour, and fifty-one against it. The Lords then went into Committee on the Commons' resolution, and at once proceeded, as was

natural enough, to dispute the clause in its preamble
which referred to the original contract between the
King and the people. No Tory of course could really
have subscribed to the doctrine implied in these words ;
but it was doubtless as hard in those days as in these to
interest an assembly of English politicians in affirmations
of abstract political principle, and some Tories probably
thought it not worth while to multiply causes of dissent
with the Lower House by attacking a purely academic
recital of their resolution. Anyhow, the numbers of
the minority slightly fell off, only forty-six peers object-
ing to the phrase, while fifty-three voted that it should
stand. The word " deserted " was then substituted without a division for the word " abdicated," and the hour
being late, the Lords adjourned.

The real battle, of course, was now at hand, and to
any one who assents to the foregoing criticisms it will
be evident that it was far less of a conflict on a point
of constitutional principle, and far more of a struggle
between the parties of two distinct—one cannot call
them rival—claimants to the throne than high-flying
Whig writers are accustomed to represent it. It would,
of course, be too much to say that the Whigs insisted on
declaring the vacancy of the throne, *only* because they
wished to place William on it, and that the Tories contended for a demise of the crown, *only* because they
wished an English princess to succeed to the throne
rather than a Dutch prince. Still, it is pretty certain
that, but for this conflict of preferences, the two political
parties, who had made so little difficulty of agreeing in
the declaration that James had ceased to reign, would
never have found it so hard to concur in its almost

necessary sequence that the throne was vacant. The debate on the last clause of the resolution began, and it soon became apparent that the Whigs were outnumbered. The forty-nine peers who had supported the proposal of a Regency, which implied that the royal title was still in James, were bound, of course, to oppose the proposition that the throne was vacant; and they were reinforced by several peers who held that that title had already devolved upon Mary. An attempt to compromise the dispute by omitting the words pronouncing the throne vacant, and inserting words which merely proclaimed the Prince and Princess of Orange King and Queen, was rejected by fifty-two votes to forty-seven [1]; and the original clause was then put and negatived by fifty-five votes to forty-one.

Thus amended by the substitution of "deserted" for "abdicated," and the omission of the words "and

[1] The offer and rejection of this compromise appears to me to be additional proof of the proposition advanced in the text — viz. that both Whigs and Tories were far more solicitous for the success of their candidate than for the triumph of their principles. Macaulay, it is true, contends, as from his point of view he was bound to do, that the Whigs made no concession of principle in proposing their compromise; for if, he argues, the Convention could elect William and Mary there must have been a vacancy of the throne. But surely the resolution as amended might have been treated as merely *declaratory* of Mary's title, and elective only so far as it associated William with her on a throne which had become his wife's by succession, and so would never have been vacated at all. No; it was a genuine and not a fictitious surrender of Whig principle; and while it proved that the Whigs were prepared to offer any such concession as would make William King, its rejection proved that the Tories cared for no such concession as did not leave Mary sole Queen. The gain of votes which the Whigs secured by the compromise probably represents the proportion of peers who really cared for the abstract principle apart from the concrete facts.

that the throne is thereby vacant," the resolution was sent back to the Commons, who instantly and without a division disagreed with the amendments. The situation was now becoming critical. The prospect of a deadlock between the two branches of the Convention threw London into a ferment ; crowds assembled in Palace Yard ; petitions were presented in that tumultuous fashion which converts supplication into menace. To their common credit, however, both parties united in resistance to these attempts at popular coercion; and William himself interposed to enjoin a stricter police of the capital. On Monday, the 4th of February, the Lords resolved to insist on their amendments ; on the following day the Commons reaffirmed their disagreement with them by 282 votes to 151. A free Conference between the two Houses was then arranged, and met on the following day.

But the dispute, like many another in our political history, had meanwhile been settled out of court. Between the date of the Peers' vote and the Conference Mary had communicated to Danby her high displeasure at the conduct of those who were setting up her claims in opposition to those of her husband ; and William, who had previously maintained an unbroken silence, now made, unsolicited, a declaration of a most important, and indeed of a conclusive kind. If the Convention, he said, chose to adopt the plan of a Regency, he had nothing to say against it, only they must look out for some other person to fill the office, for he himself would not consent to do so. As to the alternative proposal of putting Mary on the throne and allowing him to reign by her courtesy, "No man," he said, "can esteem a

woman more than I do the Princess; but I am so made
that I cannot think of holding anything by apron-strings;
nor can I think it reasonable to have any share in the
government unless it be put in my own person, and
that for the term of my life. If you think fit to settle
it otherwise I will not oppose you, but will go back to
Holland and meddle no more in your affairs." These
few sentences of plain speaking swept away the clouds
of intrigue and pedantry as by a wholesome gust of
wind. Both political parties at once perceived that
there was but one possible issue from the situation.
The Conference was duly held, and the constitutional
question was, with great display of now unnecessary
learning, solemnly debated; but the managers for the
two Houses met only to register a foregone conclusion.
The word "abdicated" was restored; the vacancy of
the throne was voted by sixty-two votes to forty-seven;
and it was immediately proposed and carried without a
division that the Prince and Princess of Orange should
be declared King and Queen of England.

It now only remained to give formal effect to this
resolution, and in so doing to settle the conditions
whereon the crown, which the Convention had now
distinctly recognised itself as conferring upon the Prince
and Princess, should be conferred. A Committee appointed by the Commons to consider what safeguards
should be taken against the aggressions of future sovereigns had made a report in which they recommended
not only a solemn enunciation of ancient constitutional
principles, but the enactment of new laws. The Commons, however, having regard to the importance of
prompt action, judiciously resolved on carrying out

only the first part of the programme. They determined
to preface their tender of the crown to William and
Mary by a recital of the royal encroachments of the
past reigns, and a formal assertion of the constitutional
principles against which such encroachments had
offended. This document, drafted by a Committee
of which the celebrated Somers, then a scarcely-known
young advocate, was the chairman, was the famous
DECLARATION OF RIGHT.

The grievances which it recapitulated in its earlier
portion, fourteen in number, were as follows:—(1) the
royal pretension to dispense with and suspend laws
without consent of Parliament; (2) the punishment of
subjects, as in the Seven Bishops' case, for petitioning
the Crown; (3) the establishment of the illegal Court of
High Commission for ecclesiastical affairs; (4) the levy of
taxes without the consent of Parliament; (5) the maintenance of a standing army in time of peace without the
same consent; (6) the disarmament of Protestants while
Papists were both armed and employed contrary to law;
(7) the violation of the freedom of election; (8) the
prosecution in the King's Bench of suits only cog-
nisable in Parliament; (9) the return of partial and
corrupt juries; (10) the requisition of excessive bail;
(11) the imposition of excessive fines; (12) the infliction
of illegal and cruel punishments; (13) the grants of the
estates of accused persons before conviction. Then, after
solemnly reaffirming the popular rights from which these
abuses of the prerogative derogated, the Declaration goes
on to recite that, having an "entire confidence" William
would "preserve them from the violation of the rights
which they have here asserted, the Three Estates

do resolve that William and Mary, Prince and Princess of Orange, be and be declared King and Queen . . . to hold the Crown and Royal Dignity . . . to them the said Prince and Princess during their Lives and the Life of the Survivor of them; and the sole and full exercise of the Royal Power be only in and exercised by the said Prince of Orange, in the Names of the said Prince and Princess during their Lives, and after their Deceases, the said Crown and Royal Dignity of the said Kingdoms and Dominions to the Heirs of the Body of the said Princess; and, for default of such Issue, to the Princess Anne of Denmark and the Heirs of her Body; and, for default of such Issue, to the Issue of the said Prince of Orange." Then followed an alteration required by the scrupulous conscience of Nottingham in the terms of the Oath of Allegiance.

On the 12th of February Mary arrived from Holland. On the following day, in the Banqueting House at White-hall, the Prince and Princess of Orange were waited on by both Houses of Convention in a body. The Declaration was read by the Clerk of the Crown; the sovereignty solemnly tendered to them by Halifax, in the name of the Estates; and on the same day they were proclaimed King and Queen in the usual places in the cities of London and Westminster.

CHAPTER VI

William's part in the Revolution—Convention declared a Parliament
—Oath of Allegiance—Settlement of Civil List—Appropriation
Clause—Toleration and Comprehension—Address of the Commons
inviting the King to declare war.

THUS prudently and calmly was effected our great
English Revolution. Both as an event and as an
achievement we have equal cause to review its history
with pleasure; for if in some aspects it testifies to the
good fortune of our nation, it reflects credit in others on
the good qualities of our people. I have endeavoured
in the last chapter to point out that the modern Whig
view of the Revolution as a great conflict between two
opposing schools of constitutional doctors, resulting in
the victory of the more liberal one, is largely legendary;
that the struggle between Whigs and Tories resolved itself
almost entirely into a dispute of preferences as between
two alternative candidates for the throne; and that both
parties showed themselves alike prepared to waive the
principles which they severally held on condition of
attaining their practical end—the success of their favoured
candidate. But this does not in any way detract either
from the value of the Revolution or from the merits of
its authors; while it otherwise only serves to conform it

to the normal type of English political work. All our great constitutional precedents are the parents of principle rather than its offspring; we deduce our theories from accomplished facts of our own creation, the creation of such accomplished facts being itself determined by no theoretical considerations, but by certain practical exigencies of the moment. Few Englishmen will think any worse of the Whig because, although firmly wedded to the principle of national sovereignty, he would have been willing to lose the opportunity of expressly affirming it so long as he could by any means place William of Orange, with full regal power, on the throne. Nor will they be any more disposed to condemn the Tory in that when he found himself compelled to give way on the practical point of the succession, he did not think it worth while to quarrel with the assertions or implications of Whig principle contained in the resolution by which the transfer was effected. On the contrary, the temper and habits of mind thus jointly illustrated are national characteristics on which we especially and not unreasonably pride ourselves.

For the purposes of a precedent, too, the transaction could hardly have come more happily off. Even a Tory of to-day will admit that it was good for the future development of our constitutional life that the Whig principles of "national sovereignty," "original contract between king and people," and all the rest of it, should then and there receive unmistakable recognition and irrevocable ratification; and this beyond question they did receive. No hair-splittings about desertion or abdication[1] could obscure the two plain facts, that the

[1] There are but two ways in which a sovereign can, while alive,

nation *deposed* James II., and by a distinct assertion of
inherent, or assumption of new, authority—it matters
not which—*made* a new king out of a man who, but for
such assertion or assumption of authority, could never
have become more than the consort of a queen.

As regards the new King himself, his behaviour at this
great crisis in his own fortunes and the destiny of two
nations deserves, at any rate, the credit of honesty and
straightforwardness.   We shall not really add to that
honour by seeking any more showy motives than those
which lie on the face of his conduct.   The mere masculine repugnance of the man of action to lower the
spear before the distaff would in any case probably
have induced him to reject the proposal of the Tory
lords.   But apart from this, his shrewd knowledge of
men and clear insight into politics assured him that he
had only to refuse the false position in order to compel
the offer of the true one.   He might have been all else
that he was—the devoted son of Holland; the true,
if unimpassioned, friend of England; the implacable
enemy of the French king and his designs; the ardent
champion of Protestantism and the liberties of Europe;
—and yet only been the more tempted in every one of
these by a place on the steps of a powerful throne, and
an influence which even from that situation he might

and *compos mentis*, become divested of his regal attributes and authority
—by abdication and by deposition ; and it is impossible to define abdication satisfactorily by any form of words which does not involve the
idea of a *voluntary* act.   Even if a voluntary abandonment or "desertion of the Government" amounted to abdication, it would not help
the case.   James's flight from England in 1688 was no more voluntary
than the flight of his brother, then king *de jure*, after Worcester in
1651.   Both flights were taken under what was or was conceived to
be *force majeure*.

have wielded to the attainment of many great ends. He was saved from accepting it solely by his pride, his ambition, and his perspicacity. He resented the thought of holding power as his wife's lieutenant, and he saw that he had only to refuse that post in order to make himself a necessity as king.

The first act of the new sovereign was to summon and swear a Privy Council, and to nominate a Ministry. In the then infancy of our modern Constitution it was not, as it now is, incumbent upon the sovereign to select the Ministers from one particular party. It was competent to him, and William deemed it expedient for him, to tender office to the representatives of both political connections. Danby, a Tory by principle, though he had sided with the Whigs in opposing the Regency scheme, and only broke away from them on the question of declaring the throne vacant, was made President of the Council. Halifax, a Trimmer indeed, but of closer affinities with Whiggery than with Toryism, and the chief upholder of the Whig doctrine on the question of the succession, became Lord Privy Seal. Nottingham, a Tory up to almost any point short of passive obedience, received the seals of one Secretaryship of State; upon Shrewsbury, a Whig, were bestowed those of the other. The Treasury and the Admiralty were committed to the Administration of Boards—the former under the presidency of Admiral Herbert, the latter under that of Charles Mordaunt, afterwards the famous and eccentric Earl of Peterborough. By an exercise of the royal authority, willingly acquiesced in at the time by the nation, but destined to entail more momentous national consequences than any of his sub-

jects foresaw, King William retained in his own hands
the exclusive direction of foreign affairs. The Great
Seal was placed in commission.

The first question propounded to the Privy Council
was whether the Convention should be declared a
lawful Parliament, or dissolved and a fresh Parliament summoned in the regular manner by royal
writ. The Council advised the former course, and a
Bill declaring the Convention a Parliament was at once
introduced and passed through the House of Lords.
It was opposed in the Commons by the Tories, who
hoped that a general election might strengthen their
numbers; but the resistance—founded as it was upon
mere technical considerations, and with historical precedent against it—was never very formidable; and the
Bill passed the Lower House in a few days, and became
law. Among its clauses was one providing that no one
should, after the 1st of March then next ensuing, sit
or vote in either House of Parliament without taking
the oaths of allegiance to the new King and Queen,
and the Jacobites and ultra-Tories conceived the hope
that many peers, bishops, and commoners would find it
impossible to reconcile their consciences to this test.
As a matter of fact the non-jurors, except among the
Episcopal body, to whom Archbishop Sancroft set the
example of recusancy, were comparatively few. Even
later, when the oath was tendered to the clergy at
large, the number of those who found themselves con-
scientiously unable to take it was but one-twentieth of
the whole body.[1]

_____

[1] This, however, it should be conceded, was really, of the two, a
more respectable proportion ; for the clergy had a sterner alternative

In the interval, however, between the passing of the Act and the day fixed for submission to the test, the great question of the royal revenues was taken up and decided. Certain proceeds of taxation were in those days granted to the Crown either for a fixed term of years or for life. The former, being on the face of them annexed to the regal office, were of course transferable without much difficulty or dispute to the new incumbent of that office ; but doubts naturally arose as to the exact legal status of the latter kind of imposts. Some were for interpreting the word "life" as virtually meaning reign, upon which construction the right to exact these taxes had lapsed by the deposition of the sovereign to whom they were granted. Others insisted on an interpretation stricter in one sense and laxer in another, and argued that though William had become entitled to these revenues as King he could only enjoy them during the life of James. In other words, in order to avoid taking liberties with the word "life," they were prepared to behave with far more unbridled license to the word "king." The practical inconvenience of settling revenues on William during the life of James may or may not have weighed more with the Parliament than the theoretical anomaly of treating the former as sovereign for one purpose and the latter as such for another ; but anyhow it was tacitly agreed to treat the grant to James as annulled by his so-called abdication. The Commons then voted the sum of £1,200,000 for the current year, one half to be appropriated to the

before them than the bishops, peers, or members of the Lower House. The latter had only status at stake—the former, in most cases, their means of subsistence.

civil list, the other half to the defences of the country —mainly, of course, in other words, to the prosecution of the impending war in Ireland. At the first sitting of Parliament, after the prorogation, which took place some months afterwards, the Royal Speech from the Throne contained an announcement to the Commons that in order that they might be satisfied how the money had been laid out which they had already given, his Majesty had directed the accounts to be laid before them whenever they should think fit to call for them. The privilege thus practically acknowledged may no doubt be, as some constitutional lawyers have contended, coeval with the constitution; but it had been so intermittently respected that its unvarying recognition from this time forward is justly reckoned as one of the chief gains which accrued to our parliamentary system from the Revolution. It seems, however, to have been only in the Stat., 9 and 10 Will. III. c. 44, that there appears an appropriation clause of the modern type apportioning all the supplies of the session to the services for which they were provided.

But while these delicate matters of royal rights and official income were being disposed of, the King was commendably anxious to show himself at once in some other light than that of an applicant for parliamentary aids. As early as the 1st of March he sent a special message to the Commons calling their attention to the "grievous burden" of the unpopular hearth - tax, and signifying that assent either "to the regulation of it, or to the taking of it wholly away," not doubting but the Commons would take care of his revenue in some other way. This judicious proposal gave great satis-

faction. The Commons replied in terms of warm
acknowledgment, and the city of London presented to
him an address of thanks. He interposed, however,
with less success and perhaps with less judgment in the
religious disputes by which the country was divided.
The traditions, alike of his nation and his house, may
well have encouraged him to aspire to the great office of
moderator and mediator between contending sects; but
it is doubtful whether such a post could under any circumstances have been within the reach of a Dutch Cal-
vinist. For the imperfect and illogically - regulated
relief accorded by the Toleration Act to most of the
dissenting denominations the country was prepared;
but neither the occasion nor the idea of the Comprehension Bill—a measure for widening the entrance to the
Church of England at the very moment when those who
had chosen to remain outside were being encouraged
by a relieving Act to remain there—was in itself a
happy one. Churchmen were, from their own point of
view, entitled to argue that the two measures proceeded
upon two opposite and conflicting theories of state
policy; that toleration, properly understood and applied,
would render comprehension superfluous, and had indeed
been accepted by the Church with that very object;
and that it was but a poor return for her surrender of
her ancient claim to compel schismatics into her
fold, that she should be required unduly to extend
its limits for the purpose of embracing them. It is
probable enough that William's eye for an ecclesiastical
scruple was not quite as keen as his insight into the
principles of civil government and the workings of
European policy, for he seems to have been surprised

and disappointed at finding that Churchmen and Dissenters, though the Toleration Act was accepted by the
former without serious difficulty and by the latter with
hearty rejoicings, would neither of them so much as look
at his scheme of comprehension. He evidently understood neither the "dissidence of dissent" nor the
Anglicanism of the Anglican Communion. The Comprehension Bill had a troubled time of it even in the
House of Lords, where it was first introduced, and after
some debate in the House of Commons it was shelved.
As vainly did William attempt to compose the feud
between the Whig and Tory Churchman and Nonconformist by offering, so to speak, a bribe to each of them
to tolerate the other. The new oath of allegiance,
framed by Parliament for itself, required to be extended
to all those classes of persons who had been compelled to
take one. Legislation was commenced for that purpose
concurrently with the debates over the Comprehension
Bill, and the King, according to Burnet, saw here, as he
thought, an opportunity of bringing the disputants to a
mutually beneficial compromise. In his speech to the
Commons on the 16th of March, he signified his wish that
in the pending legislation "they would leave room for
the admission of all Protestants that were willing and
able to serve"—a suggestion which, of course, was
directly aimed at the tests then excluding Dissenters
from office. And while he pressed this measure of
relief upon the Tories, he at the same time invited the
Whigs to make a concession to their adversaries by
absolving, as he was willing to do, the existing beneficed
clergy from the necessity of taking the new oath of
allegiance. He begged of the one party not to compel

the Nonconformist to choose between offence against
conscience and exclusion from civil office, and of the
other party not to compel a clergyman to choose between
offence against conscience and expulsion from ecclesiastical office; and he imagined that each would find their
account in consenting. But no. The Whig was determined to force the oath upon the parson; the Tory was
resolved to force the test upon the dissenter. No provision of relief for Nonconformists was introduced into
the Comprehension Bill, and the measure itself was
shortly afterwards dropped. The Oaths Bill passed in a
form which compelled every beneficed clergyman to
swear allegiance to the new King and Queen by the 1st
of August 1689, on pain of suspension, to be followed on
the 1st of February 1690, in the event of the non-juror
remaining contumacious, by deprivation.

History has done justice to these well-meaning efforts
of William; but the political virtue which for the
moment was its own reward, must, one imagines, have
been felt by him as painfully unremunerative. He could
not have expected to be personally popular, and he was
not, though Macaulay, in his desire for strong pictorial
effect, has surely exaggerated his unpopularity. But he,
no doubt, counted upon wielding a greater civil influence at the outset of his career than he in fact dis-
covered to be his, and must have learned, with some
chagrin, that he had failed to realise the vehemence of
those English party conflicts in which not even the
ablest and best intentioned of mediators can interpose
without disappointment until he has mastered all the
secrets of their intensity. On the whole, one can easily
understand the feeling of satisfaction with which he

hailed the coming of the hour when he, with whom the instincts of the European statesman and soldier were always dominant over these of the domestic administrator, was once more summoned to activity in one of the two arts in which he shone. On the 19th of April the Commons presented an address to the Crown, in which, after reciting the various acts of hostility committed by Louis XIV. against their country, " particularly the present invasion of Ireland," they assured William that when he "should think fit to enter into a war against the French king, they would give him such assistance in a parliamentary way as to enable him to support and go through with the same." To this invitation from his Parliament William returned an answer of ready acquiescence, while to those about him he exclaimed, with unwonted animation, " This is the first day of my reign."

Invasion of Ireland—Campaign of 1689—Parliamentary strife—The
conduct of the war—The Oates Case—The Succession Bill—
Attempts to pass an Indemnity Bill—Rancour of the Whigs—
Their factious opposition to William's Irish plans—Dissolution
of Parliament.

AN address from Parliament praying the sovereign to
declare war against a foreign state is far from a common
incident in our history; and even in this instance the
initiative then taken by the Commons was one of form
rather than of fact. The descent of James upon Ireland,
under the convoy of a French fleet of fifteen sail of the line,
and accompanied by a force of 2500 French soldiers,
amounted to an act of war on the part of France, if ever
such an act was committed by one nation upon another;
and it was not till more than a month after the perpetration of this outrage that the address referred to in the last
chapter was presented to the King. James landed at
Kinsale on the 12th of March; the address to the King
is dated, as has been said, on the 19th of April. England, moreover, was not the first of the coalition of
Powers which the patient diplomacy of William had
formed against Louis to take action against the common
enemy. The declaration of the German Diet had

appeared in February, and that of the States-General in March.

On the 24th of March James entered Dublin, which, in common with all the other cities of the three southern provinces of Ireland, had declared for his cause; but after only three weeks' stay in the capital it was decided, against the advice of his chief French counsellor, d'Avaux, who with the Lord Deputy Tyrconnel, and the Irish Catholic party in general, were for keeping him among the Celtic population of the island, that he should go northward and take command of the royal army in Ulster. He accordingly set out on the 14th of April, and after some further hesitations caused by conflicting reports as to the results of a skirmish between the Protestants and a body of his own men at Strabane, arrived a few days later among his troops, who were quartered a few miles south of Londonderry, a city which, with Inniskillen, had formed the rallying point for the Protestant minority when the outbreak of the Revolution, awakening the hopes of the Catholic population, appeared to threaten the "English garrison" with a repetition of the horrors of 1641. Here it had been fully expected by James's more sanguine counsellors that he would be, if not loyally, at any rate submissively received. The appearance of their lawful sovereign before their walls would at any rate, it was thought, confirm the wavering allegiance of the military under the command of the Governor, Colonel Lundy. As a matter of fact, it only served to arouse a spirit of determined resistance in the townsmen, to unite the soldiery in the same cause, and to precipitate the flight of the Jacobite governor. James and his retinue, on approaching the

gate, were fired on from the nearest bastion; a
subsequent demand for surrender was contemptuously
rejected, and after a few days' delay before the town its
rejected sovereign set off in chagrin and disappointment
to return to Dublin, leaving Londonderry to prepare for
that heroic defence of three months against the combined forces of war, disease, and famine, which has made
her name famous among the cities of the world.   James's
first act on his return to the capital was to summon
a Parliament, and a Parliament, of a sort, responded
to the summons.   That is to say, out of a hundred
temporal peers then in Ireland, fourteen, of whom ten
were Catholics, obeyed the summons, while the fidelity
at any rate of the faithful Commons was guaranteed by
the fact that only six out of the total number of two
hundred and fifty were Protestants.   Having assembled,
they promptly proceeded to attest this virtue by the
wholesale confiscation of the lands of Protestants, and
the proscription of their heads.   Ulster, however, was
still unreduced, and while that was so, denunciatory and
spoliatory decrees might well turn out to be mere waste
paper.   The dashing Inniskilleners—the cavalry, so to
speak, of that Protestant army in which Londonderry
played the part of the immovable square of infantry—had
actually meditated, though they never carried out, an
attempt to relieve their beleaguered sister city, and
at Newtown Butler they were able to render signal
service to their cause by the defeat of General Macarthy
and 6000 Irish.   By the end of July Londonderry
had been relieved; early in August Marshal Schomberg, then one of the most renowed of European
generals, landed at Carrickfergus with 16,000 men, and

it became evident even to the most hopeful of James's adherents that the northern province was lost to him irretrievably.

William meanwhile still remained in London busied with the task, at once delicate and laborious, of administering the government of a distrustful and almost unfriendly people through the agency of two bitterly divided factions. The parliamentary session had become more prolific of quarrels and more barren of counsel as it proceeded. The two Houses and the two parties had agreed with little difficulty to do justice to some of the admitted victims of the oppression practised under the last two sovereigns. The attainders of Sidney, Russell, and others were reversed without recorded dissent, but the case of Oates gave rise to acute conflict between the Lords and Commons—a conflict in which, though the conduct of the former assembly was undoubtedly arbitrary, the temper, or, at any rate, the motives of the latter appear by no means worthy of the unqualified praise bestowed upon them by the great Whig historian. Undoubtedly the Peers were without justification in refusing to reverse a sentence which the judges had solemnly pronounced illegal; but it is ridiculous to represent the Commons, as a body of judicially minded legislators, doing violence to their natural sentiments in their determination to obtain justice for Oates. Such a theory is at once refuted by the fact that, after his release under royal pardon, his personal adherents in the Commons proved numerous enough to disgrace their party and their country by procuring a pension of three hundred a year for perhaps the most infamous wretch who ever disgraced human nature. The dispute is of importance because it has

been suggested that to the bitterness of feeling en-
gendered by it was due the subsequent quarrel between
the two Houses over the succession clauses in the Bill
of Rights.   At the end of this famous enactment—the
statutory affirmation of the claims formulated by the
Convention in the Declaration of Right—it had been
proposed at William's suggestion that to the several
enumerated reversions of the British Crown a further
remainder should be added.   In the Declaration, as will
be remembered, the crown was settled, after the death of
the King or Queen, upon the survivor, and after the
death of such survivor upon the heirs of Mary, failing
whom upon Anne and her heirs, failing whom upon the
issue of William by any other wife than Mary.   It
appearing by no means improbable, having regard to the
fact that the King and Queen were childless, and that
Anne had repeatedly failed to rear the children to whom
she had given birth, that there might be a failure of
all the named reversioners, and that the otherwise legal
right of some Catholic prince might thereupon come into
conflict with the statutory exclusion of Catholic sovereigns, William proposed to entail the crown after the
last mentioned limitation upon an undoubted Protestant,
Sophia of Hanover, granddaughter of James I., and her
issue, being Protestants.   That the proposal was a well-
conceived one is evidenced by the fact that it was
actually adopted by Parliament in the succeeding reign ;
but though the Lords to whom it was submitted by
Burnet accepted it unanimously, the Commons would
have none of it.   The irritation left by the Oates quarrel
may in part have accounted for this, but Macaulay
attributes too childish a temper to the Lower House in

implying as he does that ill-humour is the sole explanation of their resistance. They in fact alleged several grounds of objection of unequal weight, but of which one at least has every appearance of *bona fides*, viz. that the mentioning of the House of Hanover would give an opportunity to foreigners of intermeddling too far in the affairs of the nation. But whatever the excuse, we can readily imagine that William regarded the action of the Commons as purely factious, and although the birth at this juncture of another son and heir to the Princess Anne deprived the succession dispute of its urgency, the cool-headed Dutchman can hardly but have been impressed with the keenness of that political strife which could keep the two branches of the legislature asunder when the cost of their dissension was the postponement of the greatest statutory assertion of their liberties since Magna Charta. For as a consequence of the irreconcilable dispute on the succession clause, the Bill of Rights had of course to be dropped; and between this date and the 20th of August, when Parliament was prorogued, the breach between William and the Whigs was still further widened by the rancour with which they pursued their political enemies, and resisted the attempts of the King to procure a statutory amnesty for past political offences. Impartiality was easier of course for him than them, but William's natural affinities of mind and politics cannot but have been rather with the Whigs than the Tories, and the steadiness of purpose with which he persisted in his patriotic though hopeless attempt at combining representatives of both political parties in his councils is, upon any view of the matter, highly honourable to him. It was the Whigs

who from the first made the experiment hopeless, and
who finally determined its failure. We owe them the
English Constitution, but we owe them also, at any rate
in the rigid inflexible shape which it has since assumed,
that *genius vultu mutabilis albus et ater*, the English
party-system.

Parliament met again after a two months' recess on
the 19th of October, and seemed at first disposed to act with
somewhat more of unity in support of the Executive.
They unanimously affirmed their determination to assist
the King in the reconquest of Ireland, and in a vigorous
prosecution of the war with France, for which purposes
they voted an extraordinary supply of two millions, a
portion of which it was at first proposed, on principles
which the enactors of the Bill of Rights (passed this
session without William's suggested amendment) had
inherited in a slightly modified form from the signatory
of Magna Charta, to raise by a special tax upon Jews.
Supplies voted, however, disunion recommenced. The
Whigs had come back from their short holiday more
bloodthirsty than ever. Beginning with a legitimate
cause of complaint against the administration in respect
of the mismanagement of the war in Ireland, where the
whole organisation of the commissariat seems to have
been almost of a Crimean inefficiency, they easily con-
verted this just grievance into a general protest against
the presence of Tories in the Government. An attempt
was made to induce William to say by whose advice he
had employed Henry Shales, the knavish Commissary-
General, to whom the scandal was mainly if not wholly
due—the object of course being to found an accusation
against some one or other of the Tory officials to whom

Shales's retention in his post was assumed to be due.
It would have been enough for William to reply that he
found the man Commissary on his accession, and simply
continued him in office.   He refused to gratify the
malicious curiosity of the address presented to him on
the subject, though he assented very readily to another
for the appointment of a commission to examine into
the state of affairs in Ireland.

The Tories were next destined to cross the sorely-
troubled king by the resistance which they offered to
him on a delicate question connected with the provision
for his sister-in-law.   On the vote of the Civil List, and
the question arising under it as to the establishment
of the Princess Anne, it had been originally proposed
by William that he himself should undertake this
charge out of his own revenues; but through the instrumentality of the Churchills a strong party was
formed among the Tories to insist upon Anne having
a settlement independent of the Crown.   Seventy
thousand a year was the (for those days) extravagant
sum which they demanded, and which proved too much
even for an indulgent House of Commons to grant.
The vote was reduced to £50,000, and though William's
dislike to the idea of a parliamentary settlement upon
his sister-in-law induced him to raise his own original
offer of £30,000 to £50,000 Anne still held out, and
a yearly income of the amount last mentioned was
accordingly secured to her for life by Act of Parliament.
In none of the parts played by the various actors in this
little political drama (the sequel to which was the
permanent estrangement of the Queen and King from
the Princess) is it easy to discern the promptings of any

public principle, or indeed of any decorously avowable
motive whatever.   The Tories would seem to have
been wholly swayed either by party and ecclesiastical
prepossessions, or by personal interests of a lower kind
—either by sentimental sympathy with a High Church-
woman, or by a practical eye to the Marlborough gold.
As to William it was eminently natural that he should
wish to retain at least *one* string of this puppet of the
Churchills in his own hands; as natural as that the
Churchills themselves should wish to deprive him of
it, and that the puppet herself should respond to the
vigorous pulling of the strings which they already held.
Neither of the two latter parties would probably have
cared to allege any public motive for their behaviour in
the transaction.   It is to be presumed, however, that
William would have done so if he could; and it is at
least noteworthy that the only objection which he seems
to have taken to Anne's parliamentary settlement affords
no logical support to his own alternative proposal.   That
Anne should have her income settled on her for life,
while his was only voted to him annually, was doubtless
a just ground of complaint; but the proper redress of
the anomaly would have been to subject his sister-in-
law's income like his own to the annual revision of the
House of Commons.   The fact that the King was dependent upon Parliament could be no reason for making
the Princess dependent not upon Parliament, but upon
the King.

Meanwhile the session wore on, and William's cherished
project of an Act of Indemnity was no nearer realisa-
tion.   He had earnestly recommended it to Parliament
in the Speech from the Throne, but nothing was further

from the hearts of the dominant party in the Commons than the idea of amnesty. They seemed bent on assuring themselves the tranquil exit of Marshal Narvaez, who died in peace with all mankind by dint of leaving himself no enemies to forgive. An Indemnity Bill was for form's sake brought in at the beginning of November, but no progress was made with it. Proscription took the place of purgation. Lords Salisbury and Peterborough, Sir Edward Hales, and others, were marked out for impeachment and summoned according to their status to the bar of one or the other House. The Lords appointed a committee to inquire into the judicial murders of Russell and Sidney, and Sir Dudley North and Lord Halifax were cited before this body to answer for their shares, real or alleged, in these dark transactions. John Hampden, a grandson of the greater John, was conspicuous for the violence of his hostility to the official Tories, and by his instrumentality a committee was appointed to prepare an address to the King to remove the authors of the late failures and to appoint "unsuspected persons" to the management of affairs. The address, however, presented by Hampden was sharply criticised for the violence of its language, and the House of Commons ultimately laid it aside. So plainly, indeed, was the Whig party now losing ground in that House, and so grave had become their apprehensions of declining popularity in the country, that with a view of at least recovering their position at the polling-booths they resolved upon one of the boldest and most unscrupulous strokes of party tactics which our history records. Into a Bill then before the House for restoring the charters to these corporations which had surrendered

them to the Crown, they introduced a clause excluding
from municipal office all persons who had been implicated in the surrenders of such charters—or, in other
words, all Tories, thus designing to fill the municipalities
with Whig office-bearers and to secure the control of the
elections to the Whig party. Smuggled into the Bill in a
House half depleted of its members by the approach of
Christmas, it needed a vigorous whip of the Tories to
procure the rejection of this clause by a narrow majority;
and William's disgust at this manœuvre was further
intensified by the attachment to his much-desired Indemnity Bill of a bill of pains and penalties against
political delinquents. So acute at this moment became
his chagrin and disappointment at the condition of
English politics that he was strongly tempted to wash
his hands of the whole distasteful and thankless business,
and he was with difficulty prevailed upon by his ministers
to abandon his design of bidding adieu to the country
which he had come to deliver and retiring to his native
land. Dissuaded from this, he resolved that he would at
least reduce Ireland to submission if he had failed to
compose the quarrels of his Parliament; and he let it
be known that he was about to quit the capital for the
headquarters of his army in Ulster. But against this,
too, the Whigs vehemently protested. An address de-
precatory of the project was said to be preparing; and
William, his patience exhausted by this last sally of
faction, determined to appeal to the good sense and
patriotism of the country.

Accordingly, on the 27th of January, after having in
a speech from the throne announced his resolve to go
to Ireland in person, "and with the blessing of God

Almighty endeavour to reduce that kingdom, that it may no longer be a charge to this," the King, to the high satisfaction of the Tories and the proportional discomfiture of the Whigs, proceeded to prorogue Parliament with a view to its early dissolution.

CHAPTER VIII

1690-1691

THE elections were contested with the utmost energy of party spirit. Both Whigs and Tories strove their hardest for the victory, but the policy of the King's appeal to the country was justified by the success of the latter. A Tory majority was returned to the House of Commons, and William felt that there was now at last a fair prospect of his effectually mediating between factions. To have replaced a party to whom he owed everything by a party who owed everything to him was undoubtedly a great step towards the attainment of his ends. He had at least secured a majority who could affect no right to dictate his policy, and had reduced those who could and did advance this pretension to a minority. His first act was to remodel his Ministry. Halifax resigned the Privy Seal, which was placed in commission; Danby, who had been raised at the distribution of honours accompanying the coronation to the Marquisate of Caermarthen, became Lord

President; Sir John Lowther, First Lord of the Treasury—not then, as now, the chief office in the Administration. Whigs and Tories were still mingled in the Government, but no longer in the old proportions.

On the 20th of March the new Parliament met, and the King addressed it in a speech in which he announced his intention of proceeding to Ireland as soon as might be, and recommended to the prompt attention of the two Houses the question of the settlement of the royal revenue and of the enactment of an amnesty. In the former of these matters their action was more conformable to sound constitutional principle than agreeable to the King. In addition to the hereditary revenues which had passed with the crown to William and Mary, the Commons would only agree to settle absolutely upon the King and Queen about one third of the fiscal revenues which had been assured to the last two sovereigns for the term of their lives. That portion of the excise, estimated at £300,000, which had been settled upon James II. for life, was now settled upon William and Mary for their joint and separate lives. But, on the other hand, the customs duties, amounting to £600,000, which had been settled for life on Charles and James successively, were granted to the Crown for a term of only four years. This restriction, in which Whigs and Tories concurred, was not unnaturally displeasing to a sovereign who justly valued himself on the ability, integrity, and thrift which made him, as he conceived, at once the most efficient and the most trustworthy steward of the national resources; but that he should have resented the action of Parliament in this matter not merely as a limitation upon the free play of his policy, but as a personal slight to himself, instructively illustrates the very limited extent to which the principles of the British Constitution, as we now know it, had established themselves in the joint recognition of the sovereign and the legislature. If there was one principle more inevitably implied in the Revolution that William had headed than another, it was that no personal claims of any individual sovereign could be allowed either to suspend or in any degree to qualify the general rule of parliamentary control. Had William contended, whether reasonably or unreasonably, that the restraint placed on him by Parliament was more severe than needed to be imposed upon *any* sovereign, his position would have been a defensible one; but his complaint, as Burnet testifies, was that the Commons were showing an undue and ungenerous jealousy of their particular sovereign for the time being. His claim to enjoy the same amount of freedom as his predecessor had abused was founded simply on the fact that James was James and that he was William; and that was obviously one of these circumstances of which the administrators of a general rule, intended to apply to any number of future Jameses and Williams, could not possibly take into account. Had this general rule been recognised with anything approaching to its acceptance in these days, it is impossible to suppose that so clear and fair an intelligence as William's could have missed its application to himself.

No doubt it may have caused him some irritation to observe with what rapidity the coalition of Whigs and Tories, which had formed for the purpose of limiting

G

his independence, dissolved again when that work was done. In a few weeks the two parties were as fiercely at odds as ever upon a Whig Abjuration Bill, the main object of which, though in one quite indefensible clause it went far beyond this, was to impose a test which the official Tories could not swallow, and so to drive them from office. It was not enough that a man should have sworn allegiance to King William; he must also expressly abjure allegiance to King James. Who knew but that he might have taken the former oath in some non-natural sense or with some mental reservations? And though the answer seemed obvious that he might take the latter in the same sense and with the same reservations, the Bill was prosecuted to its rejection in the House of Commons by a majority of thirty-three. An Abjuration Bill of a somewhat less stringent kind was then introduced into the House of Lords, the debate upon which William personally attended. He had let it be known, however, that he was opposed to the former measure, and it is probable that he had no great liking for the latter. Anyhow, it underwent so much mutilation in committee that its authors did not care to persevere with it.

The Tory majority, however, was soon after employed to an even more useful purpose in the final accomplishment of William's policy of pacification. Resolved that on this occasion the measure of indemnity should not be defeated by delay, the King submitted it personally to the Upper House in the form of an Act of Grace for political offences—a proceeding which, according to constitutional practice, abridged its deliberative stages in each House of Parliament to a single reading. Intro-

duced under such auspices, and assured of the support
of a party always dominant in the Upper House, and
now possessing a majority in the Lower, it passed
without any opposition into law, and is undoubtedly
entitled to take its place among the most honourable
and statesmanlike acts of William's career. Its value
as a political precedent was scarcely capable of exaggeration even by Macaulay; and if he somewhat inor-
dinately applauds the enlightened clemency which it
was as easy for any brave and dispassionate foreigner
to recommend as it was difficult for English parties
embittered by the mutual wrongs of a generation of
conflict to accept, it would be falling into the converse
error to insist on any serious qualification of the historian's praises. William's great qualities were his own;
they must at least divide the credit of his high-minded
and sagacious policy with the accident of his antecedents
in his own country and of his position in ours; nor
would it be gracious to attempt too nice an apportion-
ment of the shares.

Impatience to proceed to Ireland had probably something to do with the expeditious form of procedure
adopted by the King in the case of the Indemnity Act.
On the 20th of May it became law. On the same day
William informed the Houses that his departure for the
seat of war could be delayed no longer; and after having
given his assent to an Act empowering the Queen to
administer the government during his absence, he prorogued Parliament until the 14th of July. Then, having
appointed from the list of Privy Councillors a small
interior Council of Nine to advise the Queen, and having
delayed no longer than was necessary to place in their

hands the threads of a newly-discovered conspiracy,[1]
William took a tender farewell of his wife, and set forth
on the strange errand of defeating the army, if not
destroying the life, of his wife's father. "God send,"
he exclaimed, "that no harm may come to him." His
anxiety on this score for the Queen's sake was painful;
but otherwise, though he belonged to that order of brave
men whose spirits are fortified rather than exhilarated
by danger, he was cheered by the approach of the hour
of action. Ireland in the hands of a hostile army, the
shores of England threatened by a hostile fleet, a dangerous conspiracy only detected on the eve of success, a
formidable insurrection imminent in the country he was
leaving behind him, he could still say to Burnet—"As
for me, but for one thing I should enjoy the prospect of
being on horseback and under canvas again. For I am
sure that I am fitter to direct a campaign than to manage
your Houses of Lords and Commons."

On the 14th of June he landed at Carrickfergus, and
immediately set out for Belfast to take over the command from Schomberg. All Ulster rose with enthusiasm
to receive him, and the soldiers, whom treachery and
incompetency had been sacrificing by the hundred to the
ravages of disease and privation, took heart once more.
After ten days spent in concentrating his forces at

[1] The conspiracy known as Preston's—a plan of inviting the French
king to land troops in England, and offering to second his efforts by
an insurrection, and, if possible, the treacherous surrender of the
whole or a part of the British fleet. Clarendon and Dartmouth, with
other more or less eminent personages, were implicated in it, including,
at least as was suspected, the Quaker, William Penn. The conspirators were betrayed by an accomplice, and some of them sent to the
Tower. Lord Preston, a Scotch peer, a ringleader of the conspiracy,
was tried and convicted for high treason, but subsequently pardoned.

Loughbrickland, William started southward at the head
of 36,000 men.   Two days after his nephew's landing
James had left Dublin to lead his troops to Dundalk
with the view either of giving battle at that point, or
merely, as has been suggested, of eating up the country
between the capital and the invading army, so as to
impede its advance by difficulties of supply.   But if the
former were the original object of the movement it was
soon abandoned.   When William's army approached
Dundalk James fell back upon Ardee; and the former
still pressing southwards, the latter still continued his
retreat, until the pursuer was brought to a halt on the
morning of the 30th of June by the halt of the pursued,
and the English and Irish armies at last looked each other
in the face across the now historic waters of the Boyne.
Lauzun, who had succeeded De Rosen in the command
of James's forces, was a courtier rather than a general,
but the position he had here taken up, behind entrenchments and with a river in front, was strategically a
strong one—so strong indeed that the veteran Schomberg
doubted his master's wisdom in resolving upon an
immediate attack.   But William, as he had told the
Ulster men, had not come to Ireland to "let the grass
grow under his feet."   He had the advantage in
numbers; the advantage in generalship; above all, the
advantage in the quality of his troops, who, if but few
of them were as good as the trained French soldiers of
his adversary, were none of them so bad as the rapparee
Irish levies who formed the bulk of James's forces.
The day passed in an exchange of shots across the river,
from one of which William had well-nigh lost his life.
Having sat down to breakfast somewhat close to the

brink of the Boyne, he attracted the attention of the
Irish sentries on the opposite shore. Two field-pieces
were planted opposite to him, and, on his rising and
remounting his horse, were discharged at the group of
which he was the centre. The first shot killed a man
and two horses at some distance from him; the second,
better aimed, struck the river bank and grazed the
King's shoulder in its ricochet, inflicting a slight flesh
wound. His staff thronged anxiously about him, but
William, in his usual dry and stoical fashion, relieved
their fears. He was unharmed, he told them, but
"there was no need for any bullet to come nearer."
His wound was dressed, and he remained in the saddle
till nightfall. At nine o'clock he held a council of war,
and, against the advice of Schomberg, declared his
determination of effecting a passage of the river on the
following day. Unable to dissuade his master from
the rash project, as he deemed it, the veteran general
urged that at least a portion of the army should be sent
up the stream at midnight to Slane Bridge, and crossing
it at that point, should be in readiness either to
assist them in the event of their attack being unsuccessful, by a diversion in the rear of James's army,
or, in case the river should have been carried, to cut
off the retreat of the Irish by the pass of Duleek.
This plan, which, if adopted, would probably, as one
of William's biographers points out, have ended the
campaign at a stroke, was rejected: why, does not
very clearly appear. The tactics were such as might
have been thought likely to commend themselves to
William, and he could apparently have well spared the
men to execute them. It is said by the biographer above

referred to that the plan was opposed "by the Dutch
generals"; but it is not impossible that the objection
may have really come from the King himself, and have
been founded not on strategical but on political considerations.   William, as we know, was especially
solicitous about his father-in-law's life, and not perhaps
suspecting how well it would be cared for by its owner,
whom he must have remembered to have once been
brave, he may have rejected Schomberg's scheme for its
very completeness, and because he not unnaturally
assumed that in cutting off the retreat of James's army
he would be cutting off the retreat of James himself.
The too complimentary assumption that the royal general
would be last rather than first in the flight had yet to
be rebutted by events.   But whatever the reason, the
Marshal's plan was rejected; he retired, chagrined and
hurt, from the council, and the last night of the old
soldier's life was spent, it is melancholy to think, in displeasure with the master whom he had so long and
faithfully served.

The morning of the 1st of July broke fair, and a little
after sunrise the English army advanced in three
divisions to the attack.   The right under the younger
Schomberg, assisted by the Earl of Portland and James
Douglas, was detailed for the same operation which the
Marshal would have had executed four hours earlier, and
by a surprise.   Having marched a few miles up the river to
Slane Bridge, and finding there but one regiment of
Irish dragoons, they easily beat them back, crossed the
bridge, and made good their footing on the southern
bank of the Boyne.   Lauzun, apprehensive for his
command of the pass of Duleek, had detached the best of

his troops—his own countrymen—to resist the further advance of the English right ; and the centre and left of William's army were opposed at the lower fords by the Irish Catholics alone. Between them and the Dutch Guards, the French Huguenots, the men of Londonderry and Inniskillen, it was *impar congressus* indeed.[1] Schomberg in command of the centre took the water at the ford of Old Bridge. William at the head of the left wing, consisting entirely of cavalry, made for a more difficult and dangerous crossing lower down. At one point only does the passage of the river appear to have been for more than a moment doubtful. The Danes and Huguenots under Cambon and Caillemot were set upon in the act of landing by the Irish cavalry under Richard Hamilton ; the former were driven back again into the water, and the latter, unarmed with pikes, began to give ground. The conflict raged hotly for a short space at the southern exit of the ford; Caillemot fell mortally wounded ; the whole brigade was wavering; when old Schomberg, who had been watching the action from the northern bank, dashed impetuously into the river.

---

[1] James's ungenerous reproaches of his defeated troops, and the many French complaints quoted by Macaulay might not in themselves prove conclusively that the Irish showed greater *natural* cowardice, as distinguished from mere military unsteadiness, than other undisciplined levies. But the mere fact that with all their advantages of position, commanding a river which their adversaries had to cross, they made, with the exception of Hamilton's horse, so miserable an exhibition of themselves, is a clear enough indication of personal deficiencies. It is only fair to remember, however, that the generalship of James's army was beneath contempt. To leave a bridge a few miles above their position unprotected by artillery, and indeed with only a single regiment of cavalry available for resisting its being crossed by a hostile army, is surely the last word of tactical ineptitude.

" *Allons, Messieurs !* " he cried to the Huguenots, as he
pointed to the French Catholics in James's ranks,
" *voila vos persécuteurs !* " As he uttered the words a
small band of Irish horsemen came galloping in upon the
main body, the Huguenots, mistaking them for friends,
having allowed them to pass. In the confused melée
which followed the Marshal was surrounded; he received
two sabre cuts on his head, and a musket shot, said in
one account to have been fired in a fatal mistake " by
one of his own men," laid him dead upon the ground.
The arrival of William, who had with difficulty forced his
way across through the strongly flowing tide, at once
decided the doubtful struggle. " Men of Inniskillen, what
will you do for me ? " was his inspiriting question to the
sorely pressed Protestants of Ulster ; and drawing his
sword with an arm yet stiff from the wound of the
previous morning, he led his Dutch Guards and Inniskilleners against the still unbroken Irish centre. Ulster-
men and Hollanders vied with each other in steadiness
and valour ; Schomberg's cavalry came opportunely to
their support ; De Ginkell's horse effected as timely a
diversion on the enemy's left. Hamilton and his riders
being thus driven back, the heart of the defence was
broken, and after one more brief stand at Plottin Castle,
where the Inniskilleners were temporarily checked and
had again to be rallied, and where Hamilton was
wounded and made prisoner, the defeat of the Irish army
became a rout, and their retreat a flight. James, who
had watched the battle from the hill of Donore till it
went against him, had already hurried through the pass
of Duleek, and was making the best of his way to
Dublin. His army, now a broken and confused mass of

fugitives, struggled after him through the defile. The battle of the Boyne was won.

The victory, though not so immediately decisive as it might have been if Schomberg's plan had been adopted, was practically fatal to the Jacobite cause. Drogheda surrendered the next day. James, who had reached Dublin on the evening of the battle, quitted it the day after for ever. On the 3d of July he reached Waterford, whence he embarked on board a French frigate and sailed for Brest. Lauzun and Tyrconnel collected their straggling forces as best they could, and, evacuating the Irish capital immediately after James's flight, marched westward with the design of reorganising resistance at such still remaining strongholds of the deposed monarch as Limerick and Athlone.

William fixed his headquarters at Finglas, near Dublin, but enjoyed no long period of unmixed satisfaction with his victory. The day before the two armies closed upon the Boyne, the French fleet, under De Tourville, had encountered what should have been the combined fleets of England and the States off Beachy Head, but by the supineness or treachery of the English Admiral the Dutch had been left to bear the brunt of the battle alone. After hours of hard fighting they drew off with the worst of the encounter, and Admiral Herbert, destroying some of the Dutch ships, and taking the rest in tow, sailed up the Thames, leaving the enemy in undisputed possession of the Channel. The news of this defeat, and of the alarm for our unprotected coasts which it had occasioned in London, reached William on the 27th of July at Carrick-on-Suir, where he was encamped, after having reduced Waterford. He imme-

diately hurried to Dublin with the intention of embarking
to England; but, reassured by later advices informing
him that the French attempt at a descent on the Devonshire coast had proved a failure, he returned to headquarters, and hastened to prosecute the campaign.   The
glory of the Boyne, however, was destined to be somewhat
dimmed before many weeks were past.   At Limerick the
Celtic Irish showed, with the variability of their unstable
race, that they could fight bravely when "i' th' humour."
Sarsfield, left in command by the departure in disgust of
Lauzun and Tyrconnel, approved himself a leader of
vigour and resource.   He intercepted and destroyed
William's heavier battering-train before it could reach
him.   The besieged of Limerick, fighting with a desperate
courage, which even their women imitated, beat back an
assault of the English forces with much bloodshed, and
on the 30th of August, fearing the ravages of disease
with the approach of the autumnal rains, William raised
the siege of the city and returned to England.   The
campaign thus left undecided was to be taken in hand
by a greater commander than himself.   Landing in
Ireland some three weeks later, the Earl of Marlborough
gave promise of his future military prowess in the
remarkable speed and success of his operations.   In five
weeks after leaving Portsmouth he had taken Cork
and Kinsale, and had not his fast sickening army con-
strained his retirement, would probably have settled
the whole Irish business out of hand.   He returned
to London to receive from William, who, besides
being incapable of jealousy, was in the habit of
underrating his own generalship, the graceful compliment that "no officer living who has seen so little

service as my Lord Marlborough is so fit for great commands."

On the 2d of November the King once more met his Parliament, and under more favourable auspices than ever before during his reign. The imminent dangers to which the nation had been exposed had brought about a temporary truce between parties; the skill, energy, and valour with which the King had borne his part in averting them had, moreover, united them in a common sentiment of admiration and gratitude. Thanks were voted both to William, and separately to Mary, who had indeed well merited them by the spirit and vigour which she had displayed during the critical days that followed the defeat of Beachy Head. Supplies of unusual magnitude were voted with unusual readiness, and the short session, marked only by an abortive bill for confiscating the property of Jacobites, passed tranquilly away. On the 5th of January William thanked the Houses for their supplies, and assuring them, in words on which later events were to place an awkward commentary, that he would not grant away any of the forfeited property in Ireland till they had had an opportunity of declaring their wishes in that matter, he adjourned Parliament, and on the following day he quitted London to return for the first time in two years to his native country.

CHAPTER IX

Campaign of 1691 in the Netherlands—Fall of Mons—Disaffection of William's councillors—Conclusion of year's campaign—Disgrace and dismissal of Marlborough—Massacre of Glencoe.

THE night of William's arrival off the coast of Holland was wild and stormy; but impatient to be ashore, he quitted the ship which had carried him for an open boat, and after a night of extreme danger and hardship, which he passed through with his usual fearlessness and stoicism, effected a landing. His welcome among his people was enthusiastic, and his reception by the assembled notables — electors, princes, dukes, and ministers-plenipotentiary then assembled in Congress— at the Hague was signally respectful. Those among them in whom the statesman was strongest were no doubt chiefly impressed by his successful elevation of himself to a powerful throne; while to the high aristo-cratic and monarchical party among them it was suffi-cient that he filled it by a title at least good enough to relieve him of the reproach of mere high-handed usurpa-tion. Each, after his manner, did homage to the quali-ties of character, or the accidents of birth, which are respectively implied in the two meanings of the word "succeed"; over both alike, however, the ascendency of William was now in all probability much more firmly established. As wielding the power of England he was in a material sense, though not perhaps in any very imposing degree, stronger than he had been; but the accession to his moral prestige from his remarkable achievements, in the field and in the council, of the two previous years was doubtless very great. The banded enemies of the French monarch looked undoubtedly with new feelings upon the head of their coalition.

William addressed the Congress at its opening in a stirring speech in which he impressed on them the necessity of union in counsel and promptitude in action; and with such effect that the Congress resolved to oppose Louis with an army of 220,000 men, to which William, acting as his own war minister—a function which he assumed as constantly as that of the conduct of foreign affairs—engaged to contribute a contingent of 20,000. While the Congress, however, were talking their enemy was acting. A heavy blow was dealt at the confederacy by the capture of Mons, which surrendered to the vigorous siege of the French, commanded by the King in person, within a few weeks of the separation of the Congress. On the news of its danger William collected a force with all speed for its relief, but he was too late to save it; and the short period of suspension of hostilities which followed upon this disaster he took advantage of to return to England. His presence there was really more needed than he at the time imagined, for it is probable that at no time during the early years of his reign had he so much reason to distrust the fidelity of so many of his most highly placed servants. To review the intrigues with the exiled monarch, in which men like Marlborough,

Russell, Godolphin, and Shrewsbury were at this moment either voluntarily engaged, or being successfully pressed to join, is altogether beyond the scope of this volume.   But it may be worth while to interpose one observation here on what appears to me to be a common, and, in a certain sense, a mitigating feature of all these duplicities.   They differ no doubt to a certain extent in depth of moral turpitude one from another, just as the moral characters and motives of those who committed them so differed. The devouring ambition which actuated Marlborough, the disappointed Whiggism which was the dominant impulse with Russell, gave place in a man like Godolphin to mere distrust of the future, and anxiety to provide against the incalculable.   But it is only fair to recollect that this last, and for statesmen of that age, most venial motive of action, most probably played a considerable part in all their double-dealing.   None of them considered William's position assured.   All perceived that he had so far failed, and all doubted whether he would ever succeed, in winning the affection of the people.   Whether he would succeed in the experiment of governing by his factious and deeply-divided Parliament was, to say the least of it, a question of the gravest uncertainty ; and they governed their conduct accordingly. It is not necessary to suppose that because an individual statesman in William's service maintained communication with James's agents with more or less vague promises of assistance he contemplated any downright betrayal of William's cause.   In most cases his deceit was rather of that negative sort which seeks to make to itself friends betimes of the mammon of unrighteousness.   The deceiver was anxious in the event of a counter-revolution to stand well with the restored monarch, and intended no further treachery to his existing master than is necessarily involved in the attempt to serve two masters at once.

In May 1691 William returned to Flanders taking Marlborough with him. The day of that great soldier had not yet come, but though invested with no military command, it should seem that he attended councils of war where his great abilities as a general attracted the notice and admiration of experts. In June the business of campaigning was recommenced in the leisurely and ceremonious manner peculiar to the age, and with that strict attention to the limits of the "season" which in our own day is only bestowed upon the gaieties of London and the sports of the country. From early in June until the arrival of what may be called the "close-time," towards the end of September, the armies of France and of the allies continued to perform their stately military minuet to the high satisfaction of their commanders, but without suffering or inflicting on one another any serious blows.

On the 19th of October William arrived in England, and three days later he opened Parliament. The circumstances under which he met the Houses were on the whole favourable, and the mood of the Sovereign and Legislature was one of mutual good humour. It is true that the campaign in the Netherlands had been ineffectual, but its failure was more than balanced by successes nearer home. Ireland had been subdued and pacified, the navy of England had recovered its ascendency in the Channel. The King's speech to the two Houses elicited a warm reply, and the large supplies which he had still to demand for the prosecution of continental warfare was granted to him without demur. Nor was the session in other respects one of much difficulty for the King. The House of Commons indeed renewed its complaints of the magnitude of official salaries and fees, but, showing little or no capacity to discriminate between legitimate remuneration for public services and mere corrupt abuses, they naturally failed to agree upon any measure of reform. The Bill for regulating trials for high treason—a measure destined to be a subject of long contention between the two Houses—was introduced for the first time this session, and, passing the· Commons, underwent in the House of Lords an amendment to which the Lower House refused to assent. On the merits of the case it ought undoubtedly to have been adopted, but it happened to touch the royal prerogative, and the Commons made this the excuse for gratifying their not unreasonable jealousy of the exclusive privileges in the matter of justiciability which were possessed by the Peers. They showed no hesitation a little later on in making a distinct encroachment on the royal rights by imposing the salaries of the judges as a permanent charge upon the hereditary revenues of the Crown without the sovereign's consent. On this Bill William exercised for the first time his right of veto. That such first employment of it should have been on a matter touching his own interests, and at the same time affecting the independence of the judicial bench, was unfortunate; but it is impossible to complain of his exerting his constitutional authority in this case to arrest a measure of such a kind as would not, even in our more advanced days, be intro-

duced without the express assent of the Crown. The
. "event" of the year 1691 was undoubtedly the political intrigue, the discovery of which led to the dismissal
and disgrace of Marlborough. That indefatigable
plotter, who was still holding active communication with
St. Germains, undertook to move an address in the
House of Lords requesting that all foreigners might be
dismissed from the service of the Crown. It was said
and believed that his object in doing this was to inflame
the national and professional jealousies of the country
and the army against the Dutch officers in William's
service, so that in the event of William declining to
act upon the advice of his Parliament, he would find
both the people and the soldiery prepared to support
him in an ulterior design of deposing the King and
placing Anne upon the throne, with himself as mayor
of the palace. The plot, however, if plot there was,
fell through; and assuming it to have been really conceived, the natural resentment with which it inspired
William would of course sufficiently account for the
disgrace and dismissal of Marlborough which followed
immediately afterwards.[1] The attempt of the half-
lunatic, half-villain Fuller to repeat the exploits of Oates,
with a trumped-up and promptly disproved charge of
conspiracy against many prominent personages, inspired
doubts in the public mind as to whether there had ever
been any Scotch plot at all.

Here, too,—that is, among the record of the events of

[1] The whole affair is still surrounded with obscurity. At least
half a dozen conflicting explanations of Marlborough's fall are in existence, and from the same hand—that of Burnet. It cannot be said
that the conspiracy theory, which Macaulay of course adopts, is in
itself at all improbable.

the winter of 1691 and the spring of 1692,—seems the
most fitting place to take notice of a strange and terrible
incident, which, though of little importance from the
historical point of view, could on no account be omitted
from a biography of William III.   On the 13th of February 1692, at five o'clock in the morning, was perpe-
trated, under circumstances of signal perfidy and barbarity,
the crime known as the Massacre of Glencoe—the surprise
and slaughter of· the chief and thirty-eight men of the
Macdonalds by two companies of soldiers, who had been
quartered upon the clan for the preconcerted purpose of
their extirpation, under the command of Captain Camp
bell of Glenlyon.   It is not necessary, and would here
be impossible, to give more than a highly condensed
account of the intrigues, amounting almost to conspiracy, among various enemies of the ill-fated clan,
which preceded the massacre.   Suffice it to say that
private revenge combined with public policy to suggest
the act.   It was the joint work of the Earls of Bread-
albane and Argyle—hereditary foes of the Macdonalds
—and of the Secretary of State for Scotland, Sir John
Dalrymple, Master of Stair; but the order upon which
this official assumed to act was signed and countersigned
by the King himself.   It was in these words: "As for
MacIan of Glencoe and that tribe, if they can be distinguished from the other Highlanders, it will be proper
for the vindication of public justice to extirpate that set
of thieves."   The "other Highlanders" from whom they
were to be distinguished had, in accordance with a
proclamation issued in the autumn of the previous year,
made formal submission to the Government and taken
the oath of allegiance to the sovereign before the 1st of

January 1692. This, by an accident, MacIan had failed
to do. He had presented himself on the 31st of December 1691 to the officer in command at Fort William;
but, being informed by him that he had no power to
administer the oaths, the old chief was obliged to betake
himself to Inverary, to be there sworn by the Sheriff of
Argyleshire, Sir Colin Campbell of Ardkinglass, who,
although the submitted Highlander did not arrive there
till the 6th of January, consented, after some demur, to
administer to him the oaths. A certificate setting forth
the circumstances was transmitted to the Council at
Edinburgh, but was there cancelled for irregularity; and
the fact of MacIan's tardy submission does not appear to
have been—indeed, we may affirm with confidence that
it never was—brought to the knowledge of the King.
Acting, however, on the pretended authority of the
royal order, the Master of Stair gave directions to the
military authorities that "the thieving tribe of Glencoe
be rooted out to purpose"; adding in a later despatch to
the commander of Fort William: "Pray, when the thing
concerning Glencoe is resolved let it be secret and sudden;
better not meddle with them than not to purpose;" and
again, in a still later communication: "I hope the
soldiers will not trouble the Government with prisoners."
Acting on these sinister injunctions, Captain Campbell
of Glenlyon marched his men to Glencoe, and, pretend-
ing that he came as a friend and not as an enemy,
quartered them upon the Macdonalds, by whom they
were cordially received and hospitably entertained.
After a twelve days' sojourn among the clan, Glenlyon
received orders from his superior officer to proceed to
his bloody work, and at five in the morning of the 13th

of February the soldiers fell upon their unsuspecting
hosts in their sleep.   The massacre, however, was less
skilfully executed than it had been cunningly planned.
The greater portion of the Macdonalds, including the
sons of the chief, effected their escape; but MacIan
himself, with his wife and thirty-eight of his clansmen,
including some women and children, were ruthlessly
murdered.   As many more, in all probability, fell
victims to the rigours of a Highland winter in their
attempted flight.   In those days of slow communication
it was long before the story of the savage deed became
known, or at least before it was recognised as possessing
a more trustworthy character than the ordinary Jacobite
fables of the day; and it was eagerly caught up, of
course, by the political enemies of the King and the
Government.   History has acquitted William of all
complicity with the crime in the precise form in which
it was committed, as indeed it would only be reasonable
to acquit any ruler possessing, we will not say common
humanity, but the common instincts of the soldier.   But
Burnet's attempt to exonerate his master on the plea of
having signed the order of "extirpation" through in-
advertence, and Macaulay's half-suggestion that it was
his general incuriousness in Scotch affairs which made
him Stair's unquestioning instrument in the matter,
must be alike dismissed.   It was not William's practice
to affix his signature to public documents of which he
knew not the purport; and the mere fact that the
Macdonalds of Glencoe were excepted by name from
the submitted clans, and with the careful proviso that
the proposed measure should only be taken against them
"if they could well be separated from the rest," seems

to afford sufficient proof that to this particular matter of Scotch administration, at any rate, his attention was specially called.

There is, in short, no good reason to doubt that when William signed the order for the "extirpation" of the Macdonalds he meant them to be extirpated. He treated his act as equivalent to the issue of one of those "letters of fire and sword" which in those wild days of Highland history formed a recognised instrument of police. He would undoubtedly have been quite pre-pared to hear that a regiment had been marched into the valley of Glencoe, had put the contumacious clansmen (as he believed them to be) to the sword, and left their village a heap of smoking ruins. As undoubtedly he was *not* prepared to hear that a body of soldiers had quartered themselves on the clan under pretence of amity, and had treacherously slaughtered them at un-awares. But though it is likely enough that when he did hear of this he was disgusted with the unsoldierly cowardice of the proceeding, we should mistake both the man and the time in supposing that he viewed it with the horror and detestation which in our own days it excites. He regarded it, so far as one can judge, as a mere blundering excess of duty and nothing more. Four years later, when an inquiry was instituted into the matter by the Scotch Parliament, he showed no disposi-tion to press it forward ;[1] and later on, when a commission reported that the affair of Glencoe was a murder for which

---

[1] Macaulay, in that injudicious spirit of special pleading which is often so damaging to his hero, says that the King, "who knew little and cared little" about Scotland, "*forgot* to urge the commissioners." As if a king would be likely to "forget" an inquiry as to whether one of his secretaries of state had or had not been guilty of murder.

the Master of Stair was primarily responsible, he steadily declined to inflict any further penalty on the chief culprit than he had already suffered in his dismissal from office. Burnet's excuse for William that he was alarmed at finding how many men it would be necessary for him to punish for the massacre is, as Macaulay rightly says, no justification for his screening the one criminal whose case was so easily distinguishable from the others, and whose guilt was so much more heinous than theirs. It is idle, in short, to deny that in the matter of the Glencoe Massacre William incurred something of the responsibility of an accessory after the fact.

NEVER perhaps in the whole course of his unresting life
were the energies of William more severely taxed, and
never did his great moral and intellectual qualities shine
forth with a brighter lustre, than in the years 1692-93.
The great victory of La Hogue and the destruction of
the flower of the French fleet did, it is true, relieve
England of any immediate dread either of insurrection
or invasion, and so far the prospect before him acquired
a slight improvement towards the summer of 1692. But
this was the only gleam of light in the horizon; elsewhere the darkness gathered more thickly than ever as
the months rolled on. The years 1692 and 1693 were
years of diplomatic difficulties and military reverses—the
one encountered with unerring sagacity and untiring
patience, the other sustained with a noble fortitude.
The great coalition of Powers which he had succeeded in
forming to resist the ambition of Louis was never nearer
dissolution than in the spring of 1692. The Scandi-

navian states, who had held aloof from it from the first, were now rapidly changing the benevolence of their neutrality into something not easily distinguishable from its reverse. The new Pope Innocent XII. showed himself far less amicably disposed towards William than his two predecessors. The decrepitude of Spain and the arrogant self-will of Austria were displaying themselves more conspicuously than ever. Savoy was ruled by a duke who was more than half suspected of being a traitor. Out of materials so rotten and so ill-assorted as these had the one statesman of the whole group to build up and maintain the barrier which he was bent on erecting against the inroads of France. By what incessant toil and unfailing tact, with what insistences here and concessions there, with what appeals to the vanity of this potentate, the bigotry of that, the cupidity of the third, and the apprehensions of all, he succeeded in keeping them side by side and with their faces to the common enemy it would be impossible to describe, in a manner at all worthy of the subject, within the space at my command. Suffice it to say that William did succeed in saving the league from dissolution, and in getting their armies once more into the field. But not, unfortunately, to any purpose. The campaign of the present year was destined to repeat the errors of the last, and these errors were to be paid for at a heavier cost. Mons had fallen in 1691, through the delays and mismanagement of the allied armies; and in 1692 a greater fortress than Mons was to share its fate. The French king was bent upon the capture of the great stronghold of Namur, and the enemy, as in the case of Mons, were too slow in their movements and too ineffective in their dispositions to prevent it.

Marching to the assault of the doomed city, with a magnificence of courtly pageantry which had never before been witnessed in warfare, Louis sat down before Namur, and in eight days its faint-hearted governor, the nominee of the Spanish viceroy of the Netherlands, surrendered at discretion. Having accomplished, or rather having graciously condescended to witness the accomplishment of this feat of arms, Louis returned to Versailles, leaving his army under the command of Luxembourg. The fall of Namur was a severe blow to the hopes of William, but yet worse disasters were in store for him. He was now pitted against one who enjoyed the reputation of the greatest general of the age, and William, a fair but by no means brilliant strategist, was unequal to the contest with his accomplished adversary. Luxembourg lay at Steinkirk, and William approaching him from a place named Lambeque, opened his attack upon him by a well-conceived surprise which promised at first to throw the French army into complete disorder. Luxembourg's resource and energy, however, were equal to the emergency. He rallied and steadied his troops with astonishing speed, and the nature of the ground preventing the allies from advancing as rapidly as they had expected, they found the enemy in a posture to receive them. The British forces were in the front, commanded by Count Solmes, the division of Mackay, a name now honourable for many generations in the annals of continental, no less than of Scottish warfare, leading the way. These heroes, for so, though as yet untried soldiers, they approved themselves, were to have been supported by Count Solmes with a strong body of cavalry and infantry, but at the critical moment he failed them

miserably, and his failure decided the fortunes of the
day.   After a desperate struggle, in which they long
sustained the attack of the French household troops, the
flower of Louis's army, Mackay's division began to give
way.   But no effective help arrived from Solmes.   His
cavalry could not act from the nature of the ground,
and he refused to devote his infantry to what he declared
was useless slaughter.   The division was practically
annihilated.   Its five regiments, "Cutts's, Mackay's,
Angus's, Graham's, and Leven's, all," as Corporal Trim
relates pathetically, "cut to pieces, and so had the English
Life-guards been too, had it not been for some regiments
on the right, who marched up boldly to their relief, and
received the enemy's fire in their faces, before any one of
their own platoons discharged a musket."   Bitter was the
resentment in the English army at the desertion of these
gallant troops by Count de Solmes, and William gave
vent to one of his rare outbursts of anger at the sight.
We have it indeed on the authority above quoted—
unimpeachable as first-hand tradition, for Sterne had
heard the story of these wars at the knees of an eye-
witness of and actor in them—that the King "would not
suffer the Count to come into his presence for many
months after."   The destruction of Mackay's division had
indeed decided the issue of the struggle.   Luxembourg's
army was being rapidly strengthened by reinforcements
from that of Boufflers, and there was nothing for it but
retreat.   The loss on both sides had been great, but the
moral effect of the victory was still greater.   William's
reputation for generalship, perhaps unduly raised by
his recent exploits in Ireland, underwent a serious
decline.   The French were exultant at the demonstration

of his inferiority to Luxembourg, and the victory of Steinkirk inflamed the national pride to an overweening degree.

William's popularity with his own army and people, however, was at this time about to receive one of those friendly "lifts" which his more unscrupulous enemies were continually giving it throughout his life. Grandval, a French officer, undertook, at the instigation it is said of Barbesieux, the French Minister, and with the connivance of James II., to assassinate him, and set out with that purpose, accompanied by two accomplices, for the camp of the allies. Both of these men, however, appear, with an originality and independence of initiative not often found among traitors, to have played him false simultaneously, yet without any collusion with each other. Grandval had not been long in the Netherlands before he was arrested, brought to trial before a court-martial, and, on his own confession, sentenced to death. His statement, attested by the officers constituting the court-martial, was published immediately after his execution, and the world then learnt that the dying man's meditated crime was, according to his solemn asseveration, suggested to him by a minister then, and after the exposure still retained, in the service of Louis XIV.; and that James had signified to him at an interview at St. Germains that he had been informed of the "business" on which he was setting out, and that if Grandval and his companions rendered him that service "they should never want." Neither the French king nor his Minister ever made any reply to Grandval's confession; but James, though he put forth no public disclaimer, denied on this as on other occasions that he had ever participated in any of the schemes for killing William. Probably the projectors of such schemes were careful never to mention the ugly word assassination in the royal ears, so that it might always be possible for his ex-Majesty to assume that nothing was contemplated but William's "taking-off" in a less serious than the Shakspearean sense. Plots to kidnap the "usurper" were almost as commonly broached as plots to assassinate him; and it was convenient that exalted personages should be able to persuade others, if not themselves, that they were thinking only of seizing William's person when their humbler instruments were in reality bent upon taking his life.

Towards the end of October William arrived in England, and was received with an amount of popular acclamation to which the crime of Grandval had contributed more than his own military prowess. In a few days Parliament met, and the King addressed the two Houses in a judicious speech, in which he congratulated them on their great naval victory, condoled with them on their military reverses, referred with concern to the distress occasioned by the failure of the last harvest, and informed them in effect that yet more money would be required for the effective prosecution of the war. The address in reply was amiable enough, but the Parliament, as the event soon proved, was in no very manageable mood. The confusion of parties caused by William's perseverance in his well-meant attempt at mixed government was now at its height, and the state of things created was undoubtedly not favourable either to executive or legislative efficiency. An assembly divided as was the then House of Commons by two intersecting lines of cleavage, with its Whig and Tory demarcation, traversed by a cross division into "court party" and "country party," was obviously not a body likely to display much unity and vigour. Jealousy of officialism forbade ministers to reckon on the consentaneous support even of members of their own way of political thinking, while on the other hand party differences prevented the formation of a strong opposition.

The session of 1692 was, however, fruitful both in legislative achievement and in successful legislative effort. In this year was made that valuation for the land-tax, which subsisted until the tax itself was made perpetual and redeemable more than a century afterwards in 1798; and the first loan of one million sterling, contracted by the Government in the name of a National Debt, which has now increased to almost a thousand times that amount. But the measures with which the biographer of William is more directly concerned were the Place Bill and the Triennial Bill. Of both of these legislative projects I shall have more to say hereafter. Here let it be enough to note that the former was lost in the House of Lords by a majority of three votes; and that the latter after passing both Houses was held in suspense by William until just the eve of the prorogation, and then vetoed. The occasion is one of special interest to English literature, as it was in reference to this Bill that the King consulted Sir William Temple, whose strong advice to his master to assent to the Bill was conveyed through the medium of his young secretary Jonathan Swift. After making several ministerial changes, including as the most important the elevation of Lord Somers to the Chancellorship, William prorogued

Parliament, and once more, in the perpetual succession
of the toils of war to the labours of Government, betook
himself to the Netherlands. The outlook of the continental struggle had not improved; and the task before
him, both diplomatic and military, was as formidable as
ever. He had as usual petty quarrels to compose among
the allied Powers, and wounded vanities to soothe, to
animate the energies of the lagging, and to keep an eye
on the movements of the false. The effort in which he
was the least successful was the last mentioned but one;
he was unable with all his efforts to collect a force equal
to that of Luxembourg. He managed, however, to take
the field in greater strength than he had mustered on
some previous years, and as Louis had now again put
himself, with the usual elaboration of gorgeous ceremony,
at the head of his army, William promised himself the
satisfaction of looking his lifelong enemy once more in
the face upon a battlefield. Louis, however, whether
from personal cowardice or from having really contracted under the influence of perpetual adulation a sort
of religious reverence for his own life, had none of
William's military ardour. He liked directing sieges,
but had no taste for commanding in pitched battles. In
other words, he preferred those operations of war in
which the most adventurous of generals must necessarily
remain in the rear to those in which the most cautious
of generals may find himself imperatively called upon to go
to the front. He had hoped that the more agreeable form
of warfare would be provided for him, and that he
would have an opportunity of taking Liege or Brussels
as he had taken Ghent. When, however, he found
William posted in his path with a considerable if

numerically inferior army, his martial ardour underwent a rapid reduction of temperature, and he at once signified his intention of returning to Versailles. The disappointment of Luxembourg, who had assured him of certain victory over William, was aggravated by the fact that the King insisted on detaching Boufflers with a portion of the army of the Netherlands to reinforce the troops in the Palatinate; which movement having been effected, he went home to Madame de Maintenon.

Luxembourg, however, though reduced in strength, had still the advantage over William in point of numbers, and he succeeded in further increasing the disparity by a feint in the direction of Liege, which deceived William into despatching more than twenty thousand men of his army to protect that city from attack. He was thus left with only fifty thousand men to oppose a force exceeding his own by more than half. His position, however, on the bank of the Gette was a naturally strong one, and by extraordinary efforts with the spade he succeeded in adding most formidably to its strength. On the morning of the 19th of July the men of Luxembourg's army found themselves confronted by a powerful line of earthworks manned by a brave and steady foe. Relying, however, upon a numerical superiority which he rightly regarded as more than counterbalancing William's advantages of position, Luxembourg at an early hour of the morning gave orders for the attack, and the two armies closed in a struggle more bloody and obstinate than that of Steinkirk. For eight hours the battle raged fiercely along the whole line, but most fiercely round the village of Neerwinden on the English right. This, the position of most strategic importance on the

field, was disputed with extraordinary fury. Twice did
the French troops succeed in making themselves masters
of it, and twice were they driven out by the allies,
leaving their dead in heaps behind them. At last the
household troops, who had done such service at Steinkirk, were sent against this village; it was captured a
third time, and this time it was held. William weakened
his centre and left in desperate attempts to retake it,
but in vain; and at last, as the day was wearing towards
the evening, the line of the allies gave way. The French
troops poured into and over the entrenchments; the
position was captured; nothing remained for the commander of the beaten army but to arrest disorganisation
and save retreat from becoming flight. To the moral
appeal of the situation William's great nature might be
trusted to respond, and it seems to have equally stimulated his strategic capacities. The praise of his famous
opponent is sufficient testimony to his skilful conduct of
the military operation; the memory of his fiery valour
was perpetuated in the traditions of the English army.
No doubt it was from some old messmate of Roger
Sterne's that the future author of *Tristram Shandy*
gathered the materials of that vivid picture of the retreat
across the bridge of Neerspeeken which he has put into
the mouth of My Uncle Toby. "The King," Trim
reminds his master, "was pressed hard, as your honour
knows, on every side of him." "Gallant mortal," cried
my Uncle Toby, caught up with enthusiasm, "this
moment, now that all is lost, I see him galloping across
me, corporal, to the left, to bring up the remains of the
English horse along with him to support the right and
tear the laurel from Luxembourg's brows if yet 'tis

possible. I see him with the knot of his scarf just shot off, infusing fresh spirits into poor Galway's regiment, riding along the line, then wheeling about and charging Conti at the head of it. Brave! brave! by heaven! He deserves a crown!"

With Galway's regiments, we learn from the same tradition, were those of "Wyndham and Lumley." Talmash "brought off the foot with great prudence; but the number of wounded was prodigious, and no one had time to think of anything but his own safety." It is indeed pretty evident that only William's cool heroism saved his army from annihilation. Solmes, the *fainéant* of Steinkirk, was left dead on the field. Galway himself, the refugee Ravigny, was taken prisoner; Sarsfield on the other side received a mortal wound. It was by far the deadliest battle of the whole war, and it is difficult to understand why a blow so crushing should have been so slackly followed up. One cannot help thinking what a French army and a French general would have made of such a defeat inflicted upon the troops of a continental coalition on such a battlefield some hundred years later. But the terrible rapidity of those movements with which, as with hammerstrokes, Napoleon was wont to drive home the nail of victory was then unknown to warfare. Town upon town would probably have fallen after Landen had the fruits of the victory been seized, as they would have been at a later day. But, either through the indolence of Luxembourg or the comparative immobility of a seventeenth-century army, William obtained a priceless respite. He was rejoined by the troops whom the enemy had so fatally decoyed to Liege; and three weeks after his defeat he was once

more at the head of an army stronger than he had
commanded at Landen. The danger to the allied cause
was past. Luxembourg besieged and took Charleroi for
sole trophy of his great victory, and the campaign closed
for the year.

On the 31st of October William landed in England,
and prepared for a meeting with his Parliament, to
which he could hardly have looked forward with much
pleasure. He had a bad account to give and receive.
Over the whole Continent, in Spain, Germany, and
Italy, as well as Flanders, the allies had met with
adverse fortune; at sea the vast "Smyrna fleet" of
merchantmen, four hundred strong, had, through the
incapacity of our naval commanders, been surprised
in the Bay of Lagos by the combined Brest and
Toulouse fleets of France, and, its imprudently reduced convoy of twenty English and Dutch sail having
been easily mastered, nearly three-fourths of it suffered
capture or destruction. His Parliament, however, met
him as a matter of fact in a commendably patriotic
mood. William made no attempt to ignore the serious
losses which the nation had incurred by land and sea,
though of the former he said (not perhaps with perfect
impartiality towards his own tactical errors) that "they
were only occasioned by the great numbers of our
enemies, which exceeded ours in all places"; while
the latter he described as "having brought great disgrace upon the nation." And, admitting that the
charges of the war had already been very great, "I
am yet persuaded," he added, "that the experience
of the summer is sufficient to convince us all that to
arrive at a good end of it there will be a necessity of

increasing our forces both by sea and land." The reply
of the Commons was cordial, and manifested no hesitation
as to granting the increased supplies; and their patriotic
spirit encouraged William to hold his ground on a question in which the minds of the allies were just now
about to be exercised. Louis XIV., insatiable in war as
he had hitherto been, was beginning to feel that he, and
still more that France, had had enough of the struggle.
Five years of hostilities carried on in half a dozen
quarters of Europe, with a failure of the French harvest
and the vintage, had almost prostrated the country.
Distress was rife in the provinces; even that most
patient of people showed signs of disaffection. Louis
made private overtures to the States-General with the
intention, of course, of his proposals being brought to
the ear of William. Through the neutral King of
Denmark he signified his willingness to restore all the
conquests he had made during the present war, to
renounce his pretensions to the Low Countries, and
to agree that the Elector of Bavaria should have the
Spanish Netherlands in case of the death of the King
of Spain, and that the commercial arrangements of
Europe should be put on their old footing. The great
crux of the negotiations, and of all negotiations with a
similar object, was, and was known to be, the question
of the recognition or non-recognition of the *de facto* King
and Queen of England. On this question, so far as we
can now judge, the mouth-pieces of Louis gave forth an
uncertain sound. The King of Denmark told the allies
that he was making efforts to induce the King of France
to waive the demand for the restoration of James; the
French Ambassador hinted at a compromise. This, it

has been suggested, was that "James should waive his rights, and that the Prince of Wales should be sent to England, be bred a Protestant, and, being adopted by William and Mary, be declared his heir." To such an arrangement Macaulay thinks that William would probably have had no objection, but that he "neither would nor could have made it a condition of peace with France, since the question who should reign in England was to be decided by England alone." Undoubtedly William "could" not have independently assented to a condition which, to acquire the least validity, would have necessitated the statutory revision of the succession settlement, as effected by the Convention and ratified by the Convention Parliament; but there does not seem to be much evidence that he would have assented to the condition if he could. There is no trace of any endeavour on his part to sound the chiefs of his parliamentary parties on the subject, and I cannot but think it far more likely that neither in this nor in any other matter of foreign policy was William at all disposed to share any of his discretionary powers in his capacity of virtual Foreign Minister with his Parliament, so long as he could obtain what he wanted from that body without admitting it any more fully to his confidence. His rejection of Louis's overtures, including this offer of compromise, if it was made, was probably not dictated by any high constitutional considerations at all. He thought, and rightly, that pacific advances made by so haughty an enemy indicated greater exhaustion than had been suspected, and reckoning justly that another year or two of fighting would get him better terms still, he decided that another year or two of fighting there should be. The supplies had been cheerfully voted him, and that was enough. That the Parliament which had voted them had any paramount right to decide whether they would go on voting money or accept Louis's terms almost certainly never entered his mind. To suppose that it did is to attribute to him a theory of the constitution anachronistic by fully fifty years. That such a theory is more or less designedly attributed to him in the above-quoted passage from Macaulay appears unquestionable; and the Whig historian's anticipation of history in this respect is of a piece with his 'exaggeration of the permanent significance of the constitutional changes which fall to be treated of in the next chapter.

CHAPTER XI

Formation of the first party Ministry—Reintroduction of the Triennial Bill and its defeat—Of the Place Bill and its veto—Causes of the disallowance—Macaulay's account examined—Campaign of 1694—Death of Mary.

I AM now to speak of one of the most important, as it is sometimes regarded, of all the steps made under William's auspices in the development of our parliamentary polity—a step represented as even more influential in fixing and determining that system of strict party government under which the nation is thriving or declining at the present era than even the Revolution itself—the formation of the first Ministry of the modern type. "No writer," says Macaulay in speaking of it, "has yet attempted to trace the progress of this institution—an institution indispensable to the harmonious working of our other institutions. The first Ministry was the work partly of chance and partly of wisdom—not however of that highest wisdom that is conversant with great principles of political philosophy, but of that lower wisdom which meets daily exigencies by daily expedients. Neither William nor the most enlightened of his advisers fully understood the nature and importance of that noiseless revolution—for it was no less—which began about the close of 1693, and was completed about the close of 1696. But everybody could perceive that at the close of 1693 the chief offices in the Government were distributed not unequally between the two great parties, that the men who held these offices were perpetually çaballing against each other, haranguing against each other, moving votes of censure on each other, exhibiting articles of impeachment against each other, and that the temper of the House of Commons was wild, ungovernable and uncertain. Everybody could perceive that at the close of 1696 all the principal servants of the Crown were Whigs, closely bound together by public and private ties, and prompt to defend one another against every attack, and that the majority of the House of Commons was arrayed in good order under these leaders, and had learned to move like one man at the word of command."

There are perhaps not many passages of the famous history in which its author's love of dramatic antithesis has displayed itself in a statement more likely to mislead the student. Because the change which took place in the relation of Ministers of the Crown between 1693 and 1696 was a striking one Macaulay cannot resist the temptation of describing it as though it were a final one. In 1693 Ministers in disagreement with each other, in 1696 Ministers in accord with each other—the suggestion of course being that they " lived happily ever afterwards." Certainly no one previously unacquainted with the facts would suppose from this account of them that the first politically homogeneous Ministry was a purely experimental one, and that the experiment was not repeated by William, and never even attempted by his successor, under whom the old system prevailed, though with gradual modification, throughout her reign ; that on many later occasions in our history the men in the chief offices of the Government were to be found " caballing " and sometimes even " haranguing " against each other; and, in short, that it was not till far on in the next century that the idea of Ministers being men of like political opinions " bound together by public and private ties," and supported by a majority " arrayed in good order under them, and moving like one man at the word of command," became uniformly and permanently associated with the constitution. Yet this is in fact the case. The "lower political wisdom meeting daily exigencies by daily expedients" did not devise an arrangement calculated to endure for all time ; and no one ought to have been more surprised than Macaulay if it had. It met a particular exigency by a particular expedient, and as that particular exigency did not uniformly recur, the particular expedient naturally did not at once stereotype itself in our parliamentary polity. The pure Whig Government of 1696 attained the object of its formation, namely, to carry out his war policy, and passed away. William's later ministries were of a mixed character ; the ministries of Anne were partly Whig and partly Tory ; and the political unity which prevailed in the Walpole Administration was succeeded by a return to the old practice under Pulteney. It was not, as has been said, until well on in the century that it became an admitted political axiom that Cabinets should be constructed upon some bases of political union agreed upon by the members composing the same when they accept office together.

But though it is delusive to represent a mere political

experiment as the consummation of a great constitutional change, yet an experiment by which such change
was foreshadowed cannot of course be otherwise than
deeply interesting. And such undoubtedly is the character of the ministerial reconstruction which took place
in 1693. The particular exigency which the expedient
was designed to meet is almost patent on the face of the
European situation, as it must have presented itself to a
statesman of William's views and with William's policy
at heart. The one fact that the Whigs were in favour of a
vigorous prosecution of the war with Louis on its continental theatre, while the Tories favoured the husbanding
of English military resources and the maintenance of a
defensive attitude behind our " silver streak," and under
the protection of our navy, would undoubtedly have
sufficed of itself to determine William's choice of the
former party. In all other respects he probably regarded both English parties at this as at all other times
of his life with equal indifference—if indeed one should
not say with equal aversion. He could have no love
for men who, like the Whigs, regarded him as a king of
their own making, or who, like the Tories, considered
him no king, in the full sense of the word, at all.
Whichever of the two English parties were more willing
to assist his efforts for a country which he loved far
better than England was virtually assured of his favour ;
and though no doubt he believed honestly enough that
the interests not only of continental Europe, but of
insular England, were identified with those of the
United Provinces—though no doubt he honestly regarded
Holland as only the vanguard of European and English
liberties, menaced by the insatiable ambition of Louis—

yet it is impossible to credit him, or any other mortal man in the same situation, with the capacity of impartial judgment on any point at which the interests of England and those of Holland might have diverged. Nor is it, I think, unjust to add that even when the balance of English advantage might have appeared to William himself to incline somewhat against any contemplated course of conduct, he would perhaps have held himself justified in proceeding from contemplation to action. He was in all probability firmly, and one cannot say unreasonably, possessed with the idea that England was largely his debtor and the debtor of his country; and that she should, at least within reason, make sacrifices for the protection of that nation, who and whose Prince had rendered such services to her. Whichever English party showed most disposition, or rather least reluctance, to make common cause with the United Provinces in the defence of Dutch (and therefore of English and European) liberties, became thereby the party of William's choice. No doubt his gradual construction of a pure Whig Ministry was in part dictated by a desire to secure greater stability of counsel and unity of action in the House of Commons. No doubt his laudable experiment of governing by means of both parties had had results with which he could hardly have been satisfied. But he had borne for five years with the parliamentary factiousness which that experiment had undoubtedly tended to aggravate, and there is no visible reason, save that which I have indicated, for his putting an end to the experiment at this particular moment and in this particular way. He had made shift to do without a homogeneous Ministry ever since his accession.   If now he needed a Ministry which should be not only homogeneous, but homogeneously Whig, we must look to the exigencies of his continental policy for the cause.

The process, however, of replacing the Tories of the Administration by Whigs was a very gradual one, and it was not of course until it was complete that the Whig party in the House of Commons could be trusted to support the Administration, "right or wrong," as, without much suspicion of satire, we may say to have now become the accepted constitutional practice.   Nottingham and the Tory Naval administrators were the first to go, their retirement having been in the one case consequentially, and in the other directly necessitated by the narrow escape of the latter from parliamentary censure in respect of the late naval miscarriages. Russell became First Lord of the Admiralty, and with him Nottingham, who, as Secretary of State, was then responsible for the military service, was of course unable to serve.   His place, however, was not immediately filled up, nor was it till the end of the session that any further ministerial changes were made.   And this session itself was one of peculiar constitutional interest on other grounds.   In the first place the Triennial Bill, vetoed by William in the previous session, was reintroduced, and met with a most unexpected fate. It was brought in this time in the House of Commons, and passed through all its stages up to the final one without a division.   But the motion that "the Bill do now pass" was rejected by a majority of ten.   The whole affair is involved in much obscurity, and the cause or causes of the unlooked-for rejection of the measure must always remain matter of • conjecture. Macaulay declares its defeat to have been brought about by the instrumentality of the expert parliamentary intriguer Seymour; and as no House of Commons that ever lived is likely to have relished the idea of putting a term to its own existence, it is not difficult to guess the kind of sentiment to which Seymour might have appealed. But one point not unworthy of notice in the matter is that the numbers voting in the division, 146 Noes and 136 Ayes, did not together compose a very full House. They fell short by thirty-two of the numbers who voted in the division by which the second edition of the Triennial Bill, introduced in, and passed through, the House of Lords, and sent down to the House of Commons, was rejected a fortnight afterwards. In this case, of course, the adverse majority of 197 were able to allege that they were not opposing the limitation of Parliament, but merely resisting a usurpation of constitutional jurisdiction on the part of the Peers. But it should be observed that this argument does not appear to have produced many defections from the party of the Ayes. They number 127, or only nine short of their original strength ; and assuming that these nine votes were transferred to the Noes, it will still leave some forty new votes to be accounted for. It looks rather as if these were the votes of members who would have divided against the Bill if they had dared (and as they did so soon as they got a plausible pretext for doing so), but not daring, consented to assist in compassing its rejection by absenting themselves from the division.

The Place Bill, another abortive measure of this session, had a quite different history. It was introduced in much the same shape as in the previous year, and passed the Lower House substantially unchanged. In the Lords, however, it underwent a material amendment. As originally drawn it provided that no member of the House of Commons elected after the 1st of January 1694 should accept any place of profit under the Crown on pain of forfeiting his seat, and of being incapable of sitting again in the same Parliament. The Lords, while maintaining the provision for the forfeiture of the seat, introduced words qualifying the acceptor of office to sit in the same Parliament if again chosen as a representative. This amendment the Commons adopted, and the Bill thus modified, having passed both Houses, was, somewhat to the surprise of everybody and to the disgust of many people, vetoed by the King. This exercise of the prerogative was received with far less patience than on the two former occasions, and for a few days a serious conflict between the Legislature and the Crown appeared to be imminent. An address of remonstrance was presented to William, who replied in conciliatory language, but without holding out any hopes that his veto would be withdrawn. Another debate of a somewhat excited character followed, but calmer counsels than had at first found favour with the House of Commons ultimately prevailed. A motion to prepare a new representation or remonstrance was rejected by a very large majority, and the Place Bill dropped. The great Whig historian's account of the matter is that the amendment "deprived the Bill of all efficacy both for good and evil"; but that the Commons "so little understood what they were about that, after framing a law, in one view most mischievous"—namely, in respect of

its tending to keep the chief Ministers of the Crown
out of the House of Commons, "and in another view
most beneficial"—namely, as tending to keep subordinate
officials out of the House of Commons, they were perfectly willing that it should be "transformed into a law
quite harmless and almost useless"; and that William
went out of the way to veto this quite harmless and
almost useless law, because he "understood the question
as little as the Commons themselves."

This is not a very plausible theory; nor does one
well see why Macaulay should describe that proviso of
a right to re-election—which was afterwards adopted,
and which is an essential feature of our still subsisting
Act of Anne—as depriving the Bill of nine-tenths of its
power both for good and for evil. Surely both King
and Parliament might have been credited with knowing
their own business a little better than that. It seems
reasonable rather to ask ourselves whether the amendment was such as to militate in any serious degree
against the legislative object of the Commons, or in any
similar degree to disarm the objections which William
entertained to the measure. If it did neither of these
things, there was nothing paradoxical either in the Commons accepting or the King pronouncing his veto upon
the Place Bill; and it seems to me to be clear that the
amendment did neither of these things in fact. No
doubt it was desirable, from the point of view of the
majority, that office-holders should cease to sit in Parliament and become incapacitated for re-election; and
this on the abstract and general ground that such persons were not sufficiently independent to be able to discharge the functions of legislators with advantage to the

country. So far, then, as the general principle relating
to office-holders was concerned, the amendment was
opposed to the real wishes of the Commons, and had no
reason therefore to provoke the hostility of the King.
But there was a specific ground on which the House
had cause to dislike office-holders, and a specific class of
appointments to which this ground applied; and the
Bill, even as modified by the Lords' proviso, would have
limited the royal influence in respect of these appointments to an extent quite sufficient to account both for
the Commons adopting the amendment of the Upper
House, and for the King refusing his assent to the Bill.
It would obviously have dealt a heavy, though not, of
course, a final, blow to the employment of the patronage
of the Crown for the purpose of "managing" the Legislature. It would have made it a far more difficult thing
for the Court or the Government to maintain their majority in the House of Commons by what would now be
called a corrupt use of its patronage, but what was then
regarded, or getting to be regarded—at any rate by the
party in power,—as one of the legitimate arts of rule.
For whenever the Sovereign or his Ministers endeavoured
to convert a hostile into a friendly vote by the bestowal
of office upon its possessor, he or they would always have
to reckon with the possibility that the constituents of
the bought member might not care to have their interests sold along with their parliamentary representative. They might, and on a question which strongly
moved them they very probably would, have expressed
their disapproval of his conduct by refusing to re-elect
him; in which case the Government would, of course,
have found themselves at the end of the transaction with

one piece of patronage the less, but not with one vote
the more. In a word, the Place Bill, as amended by the
Lords, though it would have left untouched the power
of the Crown to bring office-holders into Parliament,
would materially have impaired its power of turning
members of Parliament into office-holders; and apparently it was only because Macaulay viewed the Bill too
exclusively in its relation to the former power, and took
no account of its bearing on the latter, that he could
have regarded it as a measure in which William had no
real concern, and which he only vetoed through some
vague dislike of it as affecting his prerogative he hardly
knew how. So far from this, it seems to me that his
objection may well have been a very definite one, and
that he perfectly understood, and was not at all disposed to undervalue, the particular exercise of his prerogative which it threatened. For whatever may have
been his original or even his persistent repugnance to the
acts of parliamentary management by means of parliamentary corruption, he had probably come by this time
to regard it as among the inevitable if disagreeable
necessities of royal and ministerial policy under the
English system of party government.

The close of this session witnessed the virtual com-
pletion of the work of ministerial reconstruction on a
purely Whig basis. Shrewsbury, who had been offered
the Secretaryship of State left vacant by the retirement
of Nottingham, after some months of hesitation accepted the office. Trenchard, the other Secretary of
State, was also a member of the Whig party. The
rising Whig financier, Charles Montague, who had
during this session devised and carried out the legis-

lative measure for the establishment of the Bank of
England, was for this service elevated to the post of
Chancellor of the Exchequer.   The Keeper of the Seal
was the Whig Somers.   The Whig Russell was First
Lord of the Admiralty.   All the important offices of the
State were now in fact in the hands of the Whig party,
and William, now fairly embarked upon the experiment recommended by Sunderland, made one last concession to his old policy of balancing one party against
the other by a liberal distribution of honours among
the displaced Tories.

The military and naval operations of 1694 were
marked by none of these successes which catch the
public eye, but the year was really one of more moment
to the history of the struggle with Louis than at first
sight appears.   Mismanagement and treachery brought
disaster on the expedition against Brest, and the disgrace
was certainly not redeemed by the subsequent bombardment and destruction of Dieppe and Havre.   But the
despatch of Russell's fleet to the Mediterranean yielded
solid gains which more than compensated for our losses
in the Channel.   Russell relieved Barcelona, blockaded
Toulon, brought the hostile Italian States to reason, and
compelled them, for the first time, to acknowledge
William's titles, reanimated the Duke of Savoy, who
had begun to think of a separate peace with France,
and, indeed, practically brought the Mediterranean
under English maritime control.   As a consequence,
our commerce, which had been declining ever since the
Revolution, began rapidly to revive.

The land campaign, though equally undistinguished
by any striking triumph, was no less fruitful in matter

for solid satisfaction. An attempt of William to carry
the war into the enemy's country was foiled, it is true,
by the skill of Luxembourg, who repulsed the advance of
the Elector of Bavaria upon French Flanders, and this
check was, of course, more important on one side than
William's capture of the inconsiderable fortress of Huy
was on the other. But in Spain, where Russell's appearance before Barcelona had compelled De Noailles to
retreat; on the Rhine, where the Prince of Baden drove
back Delorges, and established himself for the summer
in Alsace; and in Piedmont, where, in spite of the
vacillations of the Duke of Savoy, the French gained no
material advantage—the course of events, particularly as
contrasted with those of the three previous years, gave
ample justification for the words with which William
met his Parliament on the 9th of November. "With
respect," he said, "to the war by land, I think I may
say that this year has put a stop to the progress of the
French arms." Loyal addresses were returned, and
supplies to the amount of five millions were readily
voted; but, along with the Supply Bill, the Triennial
Bill was again introduced. It was probably intimated
to Parliament, through some of the private channels of
communication with the Court, that William was not
prepared to veto it a second time. The Bill was brought
in on the first day of the session, and, together with a
Bill settling the Customs on the Crown, received the
royal assent on the 22d of December. November of
1696 was fixed as the limit of the life of the existing
Parliament. The Place Bill, vetoed by the King in the
previous session, was again introduced, and with exactly
the same results as had followed the second attempt to

pass the Triennial Bill. This measure, it will be remembered, after failing to obtain the royal assent in the session of 1692-3, was defeated in the Commons in 1693-4, and so also it happened with the Place Bill. The inference which I think suggests itself in both cases is that the exercise of the royal veto, though unpopular with the country, was not by any means equally so with the House of Commons; that there were many Tories who were not particularly keen on purging Parliament of office-holders, and not a few Whigs whose zeal for the limitation of its constitutional life was somewhat lukewarm; and that both Whigs and Tories of this order were not sorry to be able to evade their party obligations to vote for these measures by pleading their unwillingness to force the King's hand, and perhaps provoke a constitutional crisis.

The day on which William gave his assent to the Triennial Bill was to him a day of grave anxiety; and a year fairly prosperous abroad and peaceful at home was to bring him ere its close the heaviest calamity of his life. The illness of the Queen, who had been for two or three days confined to her bed, was on the evening of the 21st of December recognised by her physician as smallpox. A week afterwards, at one in the morning of the 28th of December, she died. William's grief at her loss was uncontrollable, and to all but those, and they were few, who had penetrated the stoicism beneath which he was accustomed to conceal deep feelings, it must have been a strange and moving sight. He remained for days at her bedside scarcely taking food or sleep. He broke out in the presence of Burnet into passionate outcries upon his agony at the thought of losing her, and into fervent praises of her love and virtues. "He cried out," says the Bishop, "that there was no hope, and that from being the happiest he was now going to be the miserablest creature on earth. He said that during the whole course of their marriage he had never known one single fault in her; there was a worth in her which no-body knew besides himself. . . . The King's affection was greater than those who knew him best thought his temper capable of; he went beyond all bounds in it; during her sickness he was in an agony that amazed us all, fainting often and breaking out into most violent lamentations; when she died his spirits sank so low that there was great reason to apprehend that he was following her; for some weeks after he was so little master of himself that he was not capable of minding business or of seeing company."

The depth of this affection, moreover, was not dis-proportioned, as is sometimes the case in examples of conjugal devotion, to the worthiness of the object. Even Evelyn, who was shocked as a Tory and legitimate king's-.nan by the levity of Mary's behaviour (for which, how-ever, an explanation has been suggested) on her arrival at Whitehall after James's flight, affirms of her that "she was such an admirable woman, abating for taking the crown without a due apology, as does, if possible, outdo the renowned Queen Elizabeth." The comparison, ex-travagant as it may appear at first sight, is not without some justification in the spirited behaviour of Mary on the great national crisis which occurred during her hus-band's absence in the Irish campaign. It would be absurd of course to credit Mary with Elizabeth's gifts of statecraft, or with her intellectual capacity in general,

but in courage and composure in the presence of danger
she was no unworthy successor of that great queen.   In
William's passionate declarations of his debt to her there
was no extravagance at all.   To him she had been the
most affectionate, dutiful, and forbearing of wives, and
if her influence over him fell short of retaining his
marital constancy, she endeared herself more closely to
him on the side of the purer emotions by her magnani-
mous forgiveness of his errors.   It cannot but soften the
harsher outlines of our conception of William, and help
to supply that human and homely element which is too
much wanting in his character, to know that he was
capable both of inspiring and reciprocating so true an
affection as this.

CHAPTER XII

1695-1697

Campaign of 1695—Capture of Namur by the allies—Dissolution of Parliament—William's "progress"—The elections—New Parliament—Grants to Portland—The Assassination Plot—Campaign of 1696—Fenwick's conspiracy—Negotiations with France—Peace of Ryswick.

FOR some weeks after the death of Mary William's grief for her loss disabled him from the discharge of public duties. He desisted from the personal delivery of his answers to addresses from the two Houses, and though important domestic events—such as the disgrace and dismissal of Sir John Trevor, the Speaker of the House of Commons, for corruption, and the proceedings preliminary to the contemplated impeachment of Danby, now Duke of Leeds, for the same offence—took place before the prorogation, the King does not appear to have actively interested himself in them, either on one side or the other. Leeds, though he escaped the impeachment with which he was threatened, stood morally convicted of the charges preferred against him ; but William still allowed this useful and experienced, if unscrupulous public servant to remain at the head of the Council. The only mark of royal displeasure with which he was visited was his exclusion from the list of lords-justices appointed according to custom to execute the royal authority during the King's absence on the Continent.

On the 3d of May Parliament was prorogued, and on the 12th of the same month William set out for Flanders to take command of the allied army for what was destined to be the most successful of his campaigns. Luxembourg was dead, and the command of the French army in the Netherlands had devolved on a far inferior general in the person of Marshal Villeroy. William was now matched against a general to whom he was as much superior as Luxembourg had been to him, and this reversal of conditions told speedily and signally on the fortunes of the year's campaign. The prime object of William's operations was the retrieval of the disastrous loss which the allies had suffered in 1692 by the fall of Namur. On the recapture of this important fortress he now bent his whole energies. His first movement, however, was an unsuccessful one. Athlone, who had been detached with a large force to invest the city, was unable to prevent Boufflers from throwing himself into it with a strong reinforcement. The garrison now numbered 14,000 or 15,000 men, and as its works had been planned by Vauban, the greatest military engineer of his age, its defenders reckoned it impregnable. Leaving the main body of his army under the Prince of Vaudemont, who, when pressed by Villeroy, succeeded in skilfully retiring to Ghent, William, at the head of a division, effected a junction with the forces of the Elector of Bavaria and the Brandenburg contingent, and marching to Namur proceeded rapidly to invest it. Its siege was then vigorously prosecuted. Cohorn, the pupil of Vauban, and next to him in scientific reputation, was the engineer of the allies, and, thus pitted against his master, had every incitement to the exertion of his utmost skill. The trenches were opened on the 2d of July, and on the 8th the outworks of one side of the city were attacked and carried by an English force. This was the occasion on which William is reported to have exclaimed, laying his hand on the shoulder of the Elector of Bavaria, "Look, look at my brave English!" The soldier in him was far nearer to them than the statesman, and amid the smoke and tumult of that Flemish battlefield he was doubtless stirred by emotions towards his subjects which at Kensington or Westminster he had never known. On the 17th of the month, after a fierce conflict in which the attacking forces were thrice beaten back and thrice returned to the assault, the first counterscarp of the town was carried. On the 20th the Bavarians and Brandenburgers captured another portion of the outworks, and a few days later the English and Dutch made themselves masters of the second line of fortifications. Before, however, a general assault could be ordered, Boufflers, who did not consider himself strong enough to defend the town, surrendered it on terms of being allowed to retire into the citadel, for the possession of which, in its turn, an obstinate struggle began. Villeroy, now before Brussels, endeavoured in vain by a furious and destructive bombardment of that city to compel the allies to raise the siege of the Namur citadel, and Boufflers, in his last stronghold, soon found himself exposed to so terrible a fire from one hundred and sixty cannon and sixty mortars that, unless relief reached him, he felt that capitulation could only be a question of days. At this desperate juncture Villeroy advanced to his assistance, and on the 15th of August his army, 80,000 strong, was sighted by the defenders of Namur. The siege of the citadel was not for a moment intermitted; the allies stood between the fortress they were seeking to capture and the host which was marching to relieve it, equally prepared to strike at both. For three days the two armies confronted each other—three days of such anxiety as Europe had not known since the beginning of the war. Everything seemed to portend a conflict between the two great hosts—as decisive and even epoch-making a struggle as that which, after the lapse of a century and a quarter, was to be fought out on that now historic plain which the French general had skirted on his way from Brussels. But the event surprised every one and disappointed many. On the night of the 18th Villeroy unaccountably withdrew his army, and the fate of the fortress was sealed. Portland was sent to demand its surrender, but Boufflers, oppressed by the tradition that no French marshal had ever capitulated, refused to do so, and the next day, after the bloodiest assault which the history of that time records, the allies succeeded in capturing about a mile of the prodigious outworks of the citadel. Boufflers requested a truce of forty-eight hours to bury his dead, which was allowed him; and before the expiration of the time he signified his willingness to capitulate within ten days. He was informed by the Elector of Bavaria on behalf of the allies that he must surrender immediately or prepare for an immediate renewal of the attack; and thus resolutely met he yielded. On the 26th of August the garrison marched out with the honours of war, and the greatest humiliation inflicted upon the

French king since the commencement of his career of conquest was with much pomp and circumstance consummated. Villeroy and his useless army had already retired to Mons.

The capture of Namur was the greatest event of the year, and indeed of the campaign. It marked the turn of the tide in Louis's fortunes. From 1690 onwards it had set steadily in its favour, and reached full flood on the day of Landen, in 1693. The following year may be fairly taken as representing the half-hour of slack water before the ebb begins ; but in 1695 it was plain to every one that the tide was running out. No other victory was needed to demonstrate it after that of Namur, and none in fact was won. In the autumn hostilities as usual ceased, and on the 10th of October William, leaving his army in winter quarters, returned to England to be received with a too rare warmth of welcome by his people. He seized the opportunity of this burst of popular sunshine to dissolve Parliament, which had still under the Triennial Act another year of life to run. It has been suggested that he did so to put a stop to the impeachment of Leeds, but though the proceeding against the Minister to whom he owed not only his marriage with Mary, but in a great measure his elevation to the English throne, must doubtless have given him uneasiness, he had reason enough apart from this for determining the life of the Legislature. " The happy state the nation was in," says Burnet, " put all men except the merchants in a good temper ; none could be sure we should be in so good a state next year ; so that now probably elections would fall on men who were well affected to the Government. A Parliament that saw itself in its last session might affect to be froward, the members by such a behaviour hoping to recommend themselves at the next election." And though Burnet only glances at the State prosecutions as one among the causes which decided William's action, it was with no special reference to the case of Leeds. "Besides," are his words, "if the same Parliament had been continued probably the inquiries into corruption would have been carried on which might divert them from more pressing affairs, and kindle greater heats, all which might be more decently dropped by a new Parliament than suffered to lie asleep by the old one."

A proclamation was accordingly issued dissolving the existing Parliament, and summoning a new one for the 22d of November. The interval was employed by William in an unwonted effort to conciliate the goodwill of the electors. For the first and only time in his reign he set out upon a royal progress through the eastern and northern parts of his kingdom, visiting many great houses, not only of Whig, but in some cases of Tory magnates. At each of his stopping-places the rural population of all degrees from squire to peasant thronged to see him, and it seems evident that he made almost pathetic efforts to please. "The King," says Burnet, who is always an outspoken critic of his royal master, "studied to constrain himself to a little more openness and affability than was natural to him ; but his cold and dry way had too deep a root not to return too oft upon him." Neither at Cambridge in his journey northward, nor at Oxford, which he took on his return, was his visit a success. The chiefs of the younger University invited him to no entertainment ; he declined that which was offered him by the authorities of the elder. People murmured, too, at his visit to Althorp, and some remarked, no doubt with less truth than ill-nature, that the only place in which he really succeeded in making himself agreeable was at the seat of the highly unpopular Sunderland. Nevertheless, and however little these conciliatory efforts may have contributed to the result, the elections went generally in William's favour. In many constituencies Tories lost their seats, and were replaced by Whigs. The city of London, which had returned four of the former party, now sent to Parliament four of the latter. Members were in some places expressly instructed by their constituents to support the King, and to vote whatever supplies might be necessary for the vigorous prosecution of the war. The new Parliament contained about one hundred and sixty members, of whom the greater number were known to be well disposed towards the King. William had triumphantly performed a feat which, as attempted by the advisers of the sovereign, has perhaps more often been attended with disaster than with success.

On the 22d of November, the day appointed, the new Parliament met. The Commons again chose Foley for their Speaker, and the King made a long speech from the throne. The demand for supplies was still very high, but William said that as he had engaged in the present war by the advice of his first Parliament, who thought it necessary for the defence of the Protestant religion and the preservation of the liberties of Europe, and as the last Parliament had with great cheerfulness assisted him to carry on the war, so he could not doubt but that the present Parliament would be unanimously zealous in the prosecution of it, particularly since the advantages gained that year afforded a reasonable hope of future success. The Commons voted an address of thanks and congratulation upon the success of his Majesty's arms abroad, and pledged themselves to the prosecution of the war. William returned a short but suitable answer, and the business of the session began. The Legislature set to work to effect a much-needed purification of the coinage, and as the Lords had made a concession to the Commons in respect of the measure which became necessary for this purpose, the Lower House now assented to the often rejected amendment introduced by the Upper House in the Bill for regulating trials in cases of high treason, which now at last became law. But the session was not to proceed far without giving birth to an unfortunate difference between Parliament and the King. William, with that ill-judged profuseness of liberality towards his Dutch adherents, by which he compromised not only contemporary popularity but posthumous reputation, proposed to grant to Portland a magnificent estate consisting of five very extensive manors in Denbighshire. The people of the county forthwith set up the cry that the King intended to make this foreigner Prince of Wales, so far at least as he could do so by bestowing on him all that the Crown had to give in the principality. The local gentry petitioned against the grant, and an address was voted requesting the King to stop it. "Portland," says Macaulay, "begged that he might not be the cause of a dispute between his master and the Parliament, and the King, though much mortified, yielded to the general wish of the nation." It would have been better, however, if the historian had in this place added

that William forthwith made a fresh grant to the Earl
of Portland of the manors of Grantham, Dracklow,
Pevensey, and East Greenwich, in the counties of Lincoln,
Cheshire, Sussex, and Kent, together with the honour of
Penrith in the county of Cumberland, and other manors
in Norfolk, York, and the Duchy of Lancaster. As these
ancient crown-lands were far apart it could not now be
said that the King was creating a principality for the
favourite, but it removed no other of the serious
objections to the grant.

Again, however, and as before, at a moment when the
seldom very bright sky of William's popularity threatened to become seriously overcast, the sympathies of his
people were revived by his enemies. The most formidable of the conspiracies against the King's life, that
known *par excellence* as the Assassination Plot, was set on
foot, or rather revived, as the renewal of a project which
had been frustrated several months earlier by the
departure of William for the Continent—in the autumn
of 1695 ; and by the spring of the following year was
ripe for execution. Its leading spirit was one Sir George
Barclay, a Scotchman, who came over from St. Germains
with a special commission from James, which if it did
not actually contemplate, or at least expressly sanction
assassination, was, to say the least, of a dangerously elastic
character. Among those whom he enlisted in the conspiracy were one Charnock, an ex-fellow of Magdalen
College, who had been a tool of James II. in his high-
handed violation of the statutes and liberties of that society,
Sir John Fenwick, a man of good family and connections
and a noted Jacobite agitator, and Sir William Parkyns, a
Tory. The plan of the conspirators was to lie in wait

for William at a ferry on the Thames, which he was in
the habit of crossing every Saturday on his way from
Kensington to hunt in Richmond Park.   To overpower
the royal guards it was necessary to raise the number of
the conspirators to forty, among whom it was tolerably
certain that there would be at least one traitor.   As a
matter of fact there were three.   The secret was
communicated by one of these to Portland; the King,
at first disposed to make light of it, consented at last to
abandon his hunting expedition on the Saturday fixed
for the assassination, and again on the same day in the
following week; and the principal conspirators were
arrested.   Barclay escaped to France, and the Duke of
Berwick, who had at the same time been vainly attempting
to prepare the way for a French invasion by a Jacobite
insurrection, also fled the country.   William, in a speech
from the throne, made a formal announcement to the
two Houses of the detection of the conspiracy and his
providential escape; and shortly afterwards several of
the conspirators, including Charnock and Parkyns, were
tried and executed.

That the discovery of the Assassination Plot tended,
as Macaulay holds, to revive the popularity of William
may perhaps have been the case; it is at any rate
certain that on the occasion of the next difference between the King and the Legislature he proved to be
fully master of the situation.   The growing jealousy
entertained by the landed interest towards the wealthy
traders, who were now in ever-increasing numbers disputing the representation of the counties and provincial
boroughs with the squirearchy, gave birth during the
present session to a project of legislation of a highly

reactionary kind. A Bill was brought in for excluding from the House of Commons every one not possessed of a certain estate in land. For a county member this property qualification was fixed at five hundred a year, for a borough member at two hundred. Early in February the Bill was read a second time, and referred to a select committee, whose deliberations are rendered memorable by the fact that an attempt was made in the course of them to antedate an existing provision of an electoral system by about a century and a quarter. It was proposed to add a clause enacting that votes should be taken by ballot, but the proposition was rejected without a division. Duly revised by the committee the Bill was returned to the House, and it then became apparent that the pretensions of the landed interest were to meet with resistance from an unexpected quarter. The Universities of Oxford and Cambridge raised their voices against a restriction which struck at individual ability no less than at personal property, and in deference to their protest a motion was made to except the Universities from the operation of the Bill. This, how-ever, was rejected by 151 votes to 143, and a motion subsequently made to except the city of London was not pressed to a division. The Lords, from disinclination, let us charitably hope, to embroil themselves with the elective House on a matter of electoral legislation, passed the Bill without any amendment, and it came up in due course for the royal assent. It was perhaps the least invidious of all the opportunities ever offered to William for the exercise of the veto, and he very wisely resolved to stop the Bill. In spite, however, of the obviously disinterested character of the step—the measure being one which touched no royal prerogative whatever, and which he could have no reason for vetoing save that he believed its provisions to be opposed to the true interests of the country—his action did not escape challenge. An attempt was made by a section of the Tory party to carry a vote of censure upon whatever Minister had advised him to refuse assent to the Bill. The proposal, however, was not taken up by the more moderate members of the Opposition, and was ultimately rejected by the very large majority of 219 to 70—a sufficiently emphatic affirmation of the legitimate character of at least this exercise of the prerogative of disallowance. It is of course not impossible, as has been already admitted, that the recent revulsion of goodwill towards the King may have contributed to the completeness of this victory, but it seems scarcely necessary to ascribe much to the operation of any such sentiment. It is pretty clear that the Bill for the Regulation of Elections was very doubtfully regarded in many quarters of the House; and it is indeed rather surprising that in a Parliament such as that returned in 1695, with Whig influence in a distinct ascendency, it should have been possible to carry the Bill at all. It must, moreover, be remembered that even if there had been a more pronounced liking for it in Parliament itself, the measure was essentially one of that character for which a shrewd member will not venture to vote except with one eye on his constituents. Natural as it was for a country gentleman of that day to object to a Londoner coming down with a valise full of guineas to contest with him his native county or his ancestral borough, it is not to be supposed that his objection would be shared by the

free and independent electors of either constituency.
To them it might appear by no means undesirable that
"local interest" should be stimulated to judicious liberality by the competition of the open-handed outsider.

On the 27th of April the first session of the new
Parliament came to an end, and a fortnight after the prorogation William landed in Holland, whence he immediately set out to resume the command of the allied forces
in Flanders. His presence, however, was needed rather
for purposes of counsel than command; for, in truth,
the long and desperate struggle with Louis had now
reached a stage when even the most enterprising of
captains might well be of opinion that Q. Fabius was the
only general whose tactics were worth studying. At
one time it had almost become a question which of the
combatants would be the first to swoon from exhaustion;
but before William's arrival the skilful surprise and
destruction by Athlone and Cohorn of a vast magazine
of ammunition and stores, collected by the French at
Groet, had virtually decided that question against France.
England, then in the throes of a monetary crisis, was
sufficiently hard put to it to support the continued strain
of the campaign; but upon France, with three armies
afoot in three hostile countries at once, the demand was
far more terrible. She was virtually too weak to attack
in the Netherlands; and William probably saw no advantage to himself in forcing an engagement. The
summer passed away in marches and counter-marches,
and not a blow was exchanged between Villeroy and
the strategist who had plucked Namur out of his grasp
the year before. On the Rhine operations were equally
bloodless and indecisive. In Catalonia there had been

some hard fighting, and Vendome, who had succeeded Noailles, won a dearly - bought victory over the Spaniards. Throughout the year, indeed, the pen was more busy than the sword, and the straits in which Louis found himself may be measured by the energy of his efforts to detach the allies from each other. The wavering Duke of Savoy was at last definitively won over, his seduction, it is said, being finally effected by assurances secretly transmitted to Turin from the Court of Versailles to the effect that James would inevitably be restored to his throne in consequence of the extraordinary measures then being concerted for that purpose. The Duke, upon this, went on pretence of pilgrimage to Loretto, and there signed a secret treaty with France. Suspicion of his fidelity, however, soon gained ground, and in the course of the summer he threw off the mask and declared his intention, in accordance with a clause in the secret treaty, of establishing a neutrality over all Italy. To this, of course, the Emperor and the Kings of Spain and England refused to assent; but the Duke compelled them to submission by an invasion of Milan, and all Italian resistance to the French power was brought to an end. Louis at the same time made separate overtures of peace to the Dutch, and with such success that the States-General formally resolved that the concessions of France afforded good ground for a treaty. The terms were communicated to the other members of the confederacy, by some of the weaker of whom they were accepted, although the Emperor and the King of Spain united in rejecting them.

While matters were in this condition William returned to England for the parliamentary session, and in his speech on the 20th of October to the two Houses he informed them that overtures of peace had been made by the enemy. But the language in which he referred to them left no doubt of his own views. "I am sure," he said, "we shall agree in opinion that the only way of treating with France is with our swords in our hands." This is not a method of treating with foreign Powers which finds equal favour in our own day; but in 1696 there was no great difference among English parties as to the proper mode of negotiating, at any rate with Louis XIV. The House of Commons was as sternly distrustful of the French king as was William himself. Protracted and burdensome as had been the struggle, they were in no more hurry to catch at Louis's overtures than he. In their address of reply the Commons recalled the fact that this was the eighth year that they had assisted his Majesty with large supplies for carrying on a just and necessary war, and that this war had cost the nation much blood as well as treasure; but they added that the benefits procured to religion and liberty were not dearly purchased at this price, and they pledged themselves to provide not only the necessary supplies for continuing the war with vigour, but also for the payment of the public debt, which had been gradually accumulating in consequence of the deficiencies of revenue. The close of this session was marked by vehement debates in both Houses on the Bill for the attainder of Sir John Fenwick. Fenwick, who had been arrested in the previous summer, and was now lying in the Tower, endeavoured to save his life by making a confession incriminating Marlborough, Godolphin, Russell, Shrewsbury, and other Lords, whom he indicated as holding communications with the exiled king. William, however, who had long been well aware of the treason of most of these accused servants of his, declined to notice the charges, and the accuser only sealed his own doom by making them. A Bill of Attainder was brought in against him by the Whigs, and, the insufficient evidence in support of it having by a straining of the law of treason been voted sufficient, passed both Houses after a series of hot debates in which neither political party showed to great advantage, and Fenwick was executed.

Early in 1697 the long struggle between France and the allies showed signs of drawing to a close. Louis had expressed his willingness to surrender the conquests made in the war, to restore Lorraine and Luxembourg to their lawful owners, and to recognise William as King of England. To these terms William and the States-General were ready enough to assent; Spain, however, and the Emperor, raised objections; the latter, as is suggested, on account of his desire to keep up the war until the death of the ailing Spanish king, so that his own pretensions to the crown of Spain might have the support of the allied army against those of the French rival in the succession. Difficulties were accordingly raised to delay the meeting by a Congress. The Emperor proposed Aix-la-Chapelle as its place of meeting, and objected to the French alternative proposal of the Hague. It was, however, finally agreed that the representation of the allies should assemble at the Hague, while those of France took up their quarters at Delft, a few miles off; and that meetings between the two sets of negotiators should take place at Ryswick, an inter-

mediate village, in a palace belonging to the Princes of
Orange. Here accordingly they met on the 9th of May
1697, England being represented by Pembroke and
Villiers, with the poet Matthew Prior as their secretary,
and France by Messieurs Harlay, Crecy, and Caillieres.
Kaunitz and De Quiros were the respective plenipotentiaries of the Empire and Spain. A Swedish minister
acted as mediator. Like other famous Congresses before
and since, however, the Congress of Ryswick made little
progress; and after it had been many weeks in session
with no visible result, William resolved to open negotiations directly with Louis through one of his generals
commanding in the Netherlands. He selected Boufflers
as the most eligible for his purpose, and Portland
was directed to solicit a short interview. Leave to
comply with this request was immediately asked and
obtained from the French king, and several conferences
took place between the two, resulting, in less time than
the Congress had taken to exchange powers and settle
formalities of precedence and procedure, in the settlement of the basis of a treaty. Portland's commission
was couched in highly authoritative terms, and Marshal
Boufflers's report of them shows most strikingly how
commanding an influence William then exercised in
Europe, and what lofty language one of the least
assuming of men regarded it as entitling him to use.
In the French Marshal's account of his first interview
with Portland he recites an assurance conveyed to him
by the latter on the part of England, "that if satisfaction
be given him on points which concern him (the Prince
of Orange) personally, he will oblige the Emperor and
the Spaniards to make peace; being satisfied for

himself, as well as the States-General, with the offers which your Majesty has made in the preliminaries, and that if the Emperor and the Spaniards persist in refusing to make peace, he will conclude it without them together with the Dutch."[1]

The required satisfaction, however, was not obtained without some difficulty. On William's side two stipulations were made, to which Louis hesitated to assent; and neither these nor the two counter demands advanced by the French king were ultimately assented to in the form in which they were originally proposed. William required first that in the peace which was to be concluded, and by which Louis was to consent to recognise him King of England, the French king should "promise and engage not to favour, directly or indirectly, King James against him." The French plenipotentiaries at the Hague had already assented to their master engaging himself not to favour directly or indirectly "the enemies of the Prince of Orange, acknowledged King of England." William, however, desired that James should be designated by name. "It is absolutely necessary," writes Boufflers, reporting Portland's words to Louis, "for the security of the Prince of Orange, that your Majesty should engage *expressly* not to favour directly or indirectly King James *nominatim;* and" (this was the second point of contention) "that he shall go and reside at Rome or elsewhere out of France, provided he be not near enough to keep up any party in England." Boufflers added that though the first demand might be waived if Louis had any reluctance to mention James by name, and that "other equivalent

[1] Grimblot's *Letters of William III.*, etc., i. 8.

terms" might be found to give the Prince of Orange the securities he desires, yet that it was indispensable in order to remove all suspicion that the exiled king should reside out of France.

To both of these stipulations Louis demurred. It was inconsistent, he held, with his honour as a sovereign, and with his duties as a host and kinsman, to name "the King of England" in the treaty and to engage to cause him to quit France; but he offered to agree "not to assist directly or indirectly the enemies of the Prince of Orange without any exception"; and Boufflers was directed to point out that the last three words would exclude all suspicion of a restriction in favour of any person whatsoever, and in fact amount to a virtual designation of James. Upon this a further clause was engrafted by William, engaging Louis "not to favour in any manner whatsoever the cabals, secret intrigues, factions, and rebellions which might occur in England, nor any person or persons who should excite or foment them," and to this Louis, after modifying the expression "person or persons" which he regarded apparently as the equivalent of " James or James's adherents," consented. An attempt was made by William to obtain an assurance that after peace was concluded James would be "induced to resolve of his own accord" to live out of France; but Louis declined to yield even thus far, and the point was waived. William perhaps believed that he could the better afford to do so, as he proposed to make his acceptance of one of Louis's two stipulations dependent upon his obtaining practical satisfaction on this head. To the demand for the pension of £50,000, to which Mary of Modena was alleged to be entitled,

William had signified his willingness to allow her any sum to which she could show lawful claim, but it seems pretty clear that he had resolved to qualify this promise by the condition that she and her husband should quit St. Germains. The other demand of Louis—too arrogant to have been seriously urged, and in all probability only put forward ·in formal fulfilment of a promise—was that a general amnesty should be granted to all those who had followed the fortunes of James, and further, that they should be restored to their forfeited estates. To this last modest request William replied that it was not in his power to grant it since the reversal of attainder was a matter of statute and not of prerogative; to the former he replied with proper spirit that "as for the general amnesty, besides that his honour and glory demand that he shall not be forced to it by a treaty of peace, the safety of his own person requires him not to recall individuals to England whom he knows to be his personal enemies; but that as soon as he shall be acknowledged King of England, and in undisturbed possession by the treaty of peace, he will readily, of his own free will, pardon those who seem to him disposed to return with good faith and to live in quietness, behaving as good and loyal subjects." The demand was of course immediately waived, and the two Powers being now in accord, it now only remained to bring the rest of the allies into the agreement. This, however, was not to be done in a moment. Both Austria and Spain held back, and while they were hesitating new successes of the French arms brought about an enhancement of the French terms. Barcelona fell before one of Louis's armies, and the South American Cartagena before a squadron of his fleet. Upon this his plenipotentiaries were instructed to announce that he intended to keep Strasburg, and that unless his terms, thus modified, were accepted by the 10th of September he should hold himself at liberty to modify them yet further. The combined influence of the reverse and the menace, assisted by the steady pressure of William's determination, at length produced the desired effect. At daybreak on the 11th of September (1697), after a night spent in debate as to the order of procedure, the Treaty of Ryswick was at last signed as between France and Spain, France and the United Provinces, and France and England—the Emperor being allowed till the 1st of November to signify his adhesion. Two days later the news was known in England, and was there received with universal rejoicings. William, however, regarded it with no unmixed satisfaction. "I received last night," he writes to the Pensionary, Heinsius, "your letter of the preceding day, and your letter of yesterday has been delivered to me to-day by Lord Villiers. May God be pleased to bless the peace which has just been concluded, and long continue it by His grace. Yet I confess that the manner in which it has been concluded inspires me with some apprehensions for the future."

CHAPTER XIII

ONE of William's first steps after the conclusion of the peace was to appoint a strong ambassador to Versailles. Portland was selected, partly, as it is said, in consequence of his jealousy of the growing ascendency of his youthful rival Keppel in the favour of William, but much more, one may suppose, because of his force of character and intimate acquaintance with European politics. The Ambassador Extraordinary was intended, as he understood his mission, to hold his head high at the Court of Louis, and he undoubtedly did so. His retinue and equipage was of remarkable splendour, and his bearing, especially towards those who showed any sign of disputing his just pretensions, was marked by an unflinching dignity.[1] He protested bluntly against the presence of

[1] It is with a mixture of amusement and admiration that one reads in Grimblot (i. 220) the account he gives of one of his diplomatic receptions : "The King had sent the Duke d'Aumont, his first gentleman of the bedchamber, to compliment me. After this the Duchess of Burgundy sent the Marquis de Villacerf. They then began to make new pretensions, requiring me to go and meet him half-way down the

the would-be assassins of William at a Court at which he
was William's representative. He pressed for the re-
moval of James and his adherents from St. Germains ;
and on both these matters Louis, while firmly maintaining the position which he had taken up at the Brabant
negotiation, showed, nevertheless, unmistakable anxiety
to conciliate the resolute ambassador. It was not, however, to deal with points of this kind that Portland had
been sent to Versailles. Another matter of the greatest
European moment was beginning to press, and it was to
endeavour to effect an adjustment of the various conflicting interests involved in it that William had
despatched his carefully-selected emissary to the French
Court. Charles II., King of Spain and the Indies, and
last of the male line of the Emperor Charles V., was
known to be near his end, and at his death the whole of
his vast empire in the two hemispheres would pass to one
or other of two powerful reigning Houses, to neither of
which its transfer would be regarded with indifference by

steps, as I had done the former nobleman, and I refused to receive him
except at the door of the antechamber, which is at the top of the
stairs. This gave rise to a lengthened dispute, during which he was
standing half-way up the steps, and I at the top, while messengers
passed backwards and forwards between us. At length I sent him
word that, if this did not content him, it would be best for each of us to
go our own way, without my having the honour of seeing him, for that
undoubtedly I should do no more, after which he came up." Upon
this grandee's leaving another difficulty arose. Portland, although he
conducted him back to his carriage, did not wait to " see him depart,"
on which the "conductor of ambassadors " made great complaints. The
dispute as to the proper ceremony of reception was renewed by the
next arrival, when the conductor of ambassadors behaved impertinently
in public, " obliging me," says Portland, " to treat him as became a
person who has the honour to represent your Majesty," whereat the
conductor of ambassadors was " confounded and irritated."

Europe at large. The rightful heir of Charles II., if blood alone had had to be considered, was the Dauphin of France, the son of his sister, who had married Louis XIV. With the consent of her husband she had at the time of her marriage renounced for herself and her posterity all pretensions to the Spanish crown, and her renunciation was duly recorded in a European Treaty. Failing this line it would be necessary to go back another generation, and the Emperor Leopold, as the son of Charles's aunt, stood next in succession. His claim was barred by no renunciation; but it was no more likely that Louis would quietly allow him to succeed than that he would submit to the succession of a Bourbon. It was not to the interests of Europe that either House should acquire such an enormous accession of territory and power. To William it appeared at any rate intolerable that the House of Bourbon should do so, and in order to avert this calamity, as he regarded it, he took one of the most keenly canvassed steps of his political life in the negotiation and conclusion of the famous Partition Treaty. There is no likelihood that posterity will ever arrive at accord upon the policy of this famous transaction, but before even attempting to consider the unfavourable criticisms passed upon it, it is absolutely necessary to note one cardinal characteristic of its nature. To William it was avowedly and essentially an expedient adopted, to use Aristotle's expression, κατὰ τὸν δεύτερον πλοῦν. It was never regarded or represented by him as more than the "second-best" thing to be done in a case where the actual best had been rendered impracticable by circumstances beyond his own control. He knew that Louis's moderation in the settlement of the terms of Ryswick had been merely politic ; that its main object was to put an end to the war, and so to break up the forces of a coalition which both he and his rival knew that it would be a hard matter to get together again ; and that the peace once concluded, Louis would have it in his power to recruit his military strength, and prepare to take advantage of the almost daily expected death of Charles II. of Spain to carry out his long cherished design upon that kingdom. There were two ways of dealing with this situation, and two only. Either England must be kept under arms, or the King of England must "transact" with the King of France. The former of these two courses was denied him by the jealousy of his English subjects, and he was accordingly forced upon the latter. In writing to the Pensionary Heinsius he deplores the fact that he cannot "remain armed," and declares that little reliance as could be placed upon engagement with France, it was absolutely necessary that such should be concluded ; since otherwise, he writes, "I do not see a possibility of preventing France from putting herself in immediate possession of the monarchy of Spain in case the King should happen to die soon." Obviously, therefore, it would be unfair to judge of the First Partition Treaty as though the arrangement of it had been deliberately selected by William from a variety of more or less eligible expedients. The only mode in which it can be logically or reasonably attacked is by contending either that the object of the Treaty, the exclusion of the grandson of Louis from the throne of Spain, was not a political end of such importance as to be worth bargaining for at all, or else that the particular bargain to which William agreed was in itself an improvident one.

So much premised, let us proceed to examine the provisions of this memorable instrument. Roughly speaking they would have effected a division of the heritage of the Spanish king between the Electoral Prince of Bavaria and the Dauphin of France. The former was to have the kingdom of Spain, the Spanish Netherlands, and the Spanish possessions in the New World; to the latter were to pass the two Sicilies and Sardinia, certain places on and off the coast of Tuscany, and the Cis-Pyrenæan portion of the Province of Guipuzcoa. Milan was to go to the Archduke Charles, the second son of the Emperor Leopold. Such was the arrangement, and whether its terms were to be deemed good or bad for England, it is at least certain that they were only obtained from the French king after long and obstinate diplomatic haggling, first between Portland, William's Ambassador-Extraordinary at Versailles, and the French Ministers, and afterwards between the Count de Tallard, Louis XIV.'s ambassador to England, and William himself. The French king was extremely anxious to secure the Spanish kingdom for his grandson Philip, Duke of Anjou, and was ready to undertake that the Dauphin and Philip's elder brother should waive their rights, so as to guard against the possibility of the French and Spanish monarchies being united under one sceptre. As to the danger lest a Bourbon, once established at Madrid, might hand over the Spanish Netherlands to the head of the family, Louis was willing to protect England and Holland against that danger by consenting that those provinces should be ceded to the Elector of Bavaria. William met this proposal, not by a direct negative, but by raising his terms of assent to it. Not only, he insisted, must the Spanish Netherlands pass to the Elector of Bavaria, but Louis must give up some fortified towns on his Flemish frontier, for the better self-protection of the United Provinces, while England was "compensated" on the Mediterranean and the Gulf of Mexico. Louis protested on his own behalf against the former of these proposals, and declared that the Spaniards would never consent to the latter. At last, unable to obtain his way with regard to the elevation of one of his grandsons to the Spanish throne, he assented to the only alternative arrangement which would prevent Spain from passing to his rival the Emperor, and signified his willingness to accept the Electoral Prince of Bavaria as the heir to the Peninsula. The obstinacy with which the points of this treaty were contested may be measured by the fact that the first interview between Pomponne and Portland, in which the matter of the Spanish succession was broached, took place on the 15th of March, and it was not till the 4th of September that the treaty was signed. It cannot therefore be contended that William spared pains to obtain what he considered the best terms from Louis, and having regard to the fact that the King of Spain was not expected to live out the year, it is plain enough that on one assumption—that, namely, of the paramount necessity of preventing the accession of a grandson of Louis to the Spanish throne—the negotiations could not with safety have been protracted much longer. The latter, in short, of the two questions which were propounded at the outset of the examination

may be said to depend for its answer upon the former.
Supposing that the exclusion of the Duke of Anjou or
the Duke of Berry from the throne of Spain was a
political object worth bargaining for at all, William cannot,
I think, be charged with having paid an improvident price
for it. Nor does it appear to me reasonably arguable
that the object in question was not worth bargaining to
obtain. It has been urged by some critics of this
transaction that the apprehensions roused in those days
at the prospect of a Bourbon prince succeeding to the
throne of Charles were exaggerated; that experience
has shown the fallacy of supposing that ties of kindred
count for much in determining the policy of monarchs,
and that it would certainly have been better that the
Spanish throne should pass to the descendant of a French
king than that the two Sicilies and other points of vantage on the Mediterranean should pass to a future French
king himself. But those who so argue rely too much upon
general principles and pay too little attention to the facts
of the particular case. One might readily admit that
ties of kindred count for little in determining the
policy of monarchs, and at the same 'time retain the
full conviction that the subsistence of the relation of
grandfather and grandson between the then King of
France—the man and the circumstances being what they
were—and the King of Spain would have been fraught
with the most disastrous consequences for all Europe.
There could be no serious doubt that the Duke of Anjou
or the Duke of Berry would be a mere puppet with his
strings pulled from beyond the Pyrenees, and that the
whole resources of his kingdom would at once have
been drawn upon by Louis to enable him to resume the

war. Had the French crown rested upon another head, or even had there been any probability that the new occupant of the Spanish throne would have time allowed him to outgrow the *regni novitas* and strike out a policy of his own, the case would have been different. But we must judge of the situation by the light of the facts as they were. It is beside the point to argue that because a grandson of Louis after all succeeded the Spanish king, and after a desolating war for his dethronement continued to reign over Spain, and his children after him, without Europe being "a penny the worse"—it is beside the point, I say, to argue that an arrangement which operated not amiss for Europe from 1712 onwards would have been tolerable in 1698. Philip V. was well enough as a king of Spain, after his grandfather's power had been brought low by a dozen more years of European war, but Philip of Anjou, the nominee and instrument of Louis XIV., at the close of the previous century, would have been a weapon pointed at the breast of free and Protestant Europe. You cannot judge of the strength or keenness of a dagger by merely estimating its power in the grasp of a failing hand.

Doubtless, however, the complaints both contemporary and subsequent of the provisions of the Partition Treaty were to some extent stimulated by the circumstances of its arrangement. It is well known that William, acting as his own Foreign Minister, carried his official independence so far as to conduct the whole of the negotiations with Louis from beginning to end without any reference to, or at least any effective consultation of, a single English Minister. Somers, it is true, had been told before the King's departure for Loo that Lord Portland had been sounded by Louis with reference to an agreement with England concerning the Spanish succession; but it was not till the terms were actually arranged that William wrote to Somers for his opinion upon them, "leaving it to his judgment to whom else he might think it proper to impart them," and adding "if it be fit that this negotiation be carried on there is no time to be lost, and you will send me the full powers under the Great Seal, with the names in blank, to treat with Count Tallard." Portland at the same time communicated directly with Vernon, the then Secretary of State, whose consent was necessary to the imprint of the Great Seal; and Somers himself confided the affair to several other Ministers. But it is clear, not only from Somers's own reply to William, but generally on the face of the whole transaction, that even if the King's English Ministers had been competent to revise the agreement, their suggestions would have come too late. Somers's criticisms, though sensible in themselves, were of the most tentative character; he excuses himself indeed that his thoughts were so ill put together, and pleaded the known effect of the waters at Tunbridge Wells, where he then was, in "discomposing and disturbing the head so as almost totally to disable one from writing"; but in fact he writes with the extreme diffidence natural to the "layman" conscious of his incapacity to advise the expert. The commission of plenipotentiaries was then drawn out by Secretary Vernon with the names left in blank, and the Chancellor requested the Secretary for his warrant before affixing the Great Seal. This, however, Vernon refused to give, and Somers thereupon sealed the powers with his own hand, taking care, however, to keep the King's letter as a

justification or an excuse for the act. That the whole
proceeding was unconstitutional, according to the fully
developed theory of the constitution, is of course obvious,
and it is only a partial and not a complete defence of
William's share in it that the theory in question was
nothing like so fully developed or so firmly established
as it is at the present day. It is all very well to say
that "William was his own Foreign Minister,"—a statement which is repeated by Whig writers, as though it
sufficed to explain any conceivable irregularity,—but
the mere fact of his being unable to complete the legal
execution of a treaty without calling in the assistance of
a Minister (or rather, as it really should have been, if the
Chancellor had not taken upon him to dispense with the
Secretary's co-operation, of two Ministers), must have been
a sufficient indication to the King of the even *then* constitutional limits of his prerogative. The *form*, in short,
was eloquent of the *fact*. It would have been plainly
irrational to suppose that the royal treaty-making
power would have been made exercisable only under the
authority of an instrument validated by an act which none
but a Minister or Ministers could perform, unless it were
intended that such Minister or Ministers should be as fully
responsible for the doings of the executive in foreign as
in domestic affairs. And assuredly it cannot be regarded
as more than a colourable recognition of this responsibility
to procure the merely mechanical assent of Ministers to
the results of an international agreement, in the
negotiations for which they have not been permitted to
take any part. It seems difficult therefore to contend
that William was not in this matter *knowingly* over-riding
constitutional restrictions, under the conviction probably

that the pressing nature of the emergency, and the danger of delaying the Spanish settlement by deliberations with the English Ministers, sufficiently justified the irregularity.

There was that, too, in Somers's letter which would have confirmed him in the belief that he had done well in agreeing betimes with his adversary. The Chancellor spoke of the "deadness and want of spirit" universally prevailing in the nation. None, he said, were disposed to the thought of entering on a new war; but all seemed to be tired out with taxes, to a degree beyond what was discerned till it appeared upon the occasion of the late elections. And, indeed, the lesson of these elections was too significant to be missed. A great change had passed over the mind of the country since the return of the Parliament of 1695, and the overthrow of the Tory ascendency by an electorate thoroughly roused to a sense of the duty of prosecuting the war, and to that end supporting the war party. In 1698, although the Tory ranks were not very largely recruited, nor those of the non-Ministerial Whigs materially reduced, it is certain that many candidates on both sides had been compelled to pledge themselves to a policy of peace and retrenchment. The new Parliament was opened by the King on the 6th of December, and the temper of the House of Commons was not long in declaring itself. The Ministerial party succeeded in carrying the election of their Speaker, Sir Thomas Littleton, but they were utterly powerless to sustain their master's military policy against the mass of opposition which it had to encounter. A resolution was adopted cutting down the army to 7000 men, "and these to consist of his Majesty's natural-born subjects." To William, whose Ministers had held out hopes to him that a force of at least 10,000 men would be sanctioned by Parliament, and who personally held that anything less than double that number would be insufficient, a resolution which would not only have inexcusably weakened, in his opinion, the defences of England, but have deprived him even of the services of those Dutch Guards who had fought with such signal bravery for the liberties of that country, caused natural and bitter chagrin. He gave the royal assent to the Bill founded upon this resolution, but he gave it in a speech through the dignified composure of which his grave concern and disappointment perceptibly struggle. A later attempt to save his Dutch Guards, almost pathetic in its character,[1] proved unsuccessful; and when, in reply to this appeal, the Commons reminded him that he had promised in 1688 to "send all foreign troops that came over with him back again," so narrow and un- generous an insistence on the strict letter of his pledge must no doubt have added to his mortification.

The occasion of this second attempt was an event to be shortly noticed, which might have been thought likely to dispose the Parliament to a more liberal view of military necessities; and William has been censured by his greatest admirer for not having applied to the House for an increase of the English establishment instead of striving to retain a force of his countrymen.

[1] The message from the King runs thus : " His Majesty is pleased to let the House know that the necessary preparations are made for transporting the Guards who came with him into England, and that he intends to send them away immediately, unless out of consideration for him the House be disposed to find a way for continuing them longer in his service, which his Majesty would take very kindly."

It is not a matter for regret, however, that this mistake, if mistake it was, should have been committed; for it enables us pretty accurately to measure the respective proportions of reason and prejudice in the conduct of Parliament. So far as the motive of the House of Commons in these military retrenchments was a purely economical one—so far even as it implied blindness to those European considerations which our insular position no more absolved us from regarding in 1698 than it does to-day—this motive was, if mistaken, respectable. Even that exaggerated dread of a standing army, which, no doubt, had more to do with the decision of the parliamentary majority than any theory, good, bad, or indifferent, of the probable course of European affairs, would not deserve to be severely judged. But it is difficult to attribute the refusal of the House of Commons to sanction William's retention of his body-guard to any worthier motive than mere jealousy of the foreigner. It was a step as unwise from the political point of view, and in its bearing on the relations of sovereign and subject, as on the moral side it was ungracious. One can well understand that the personal affront involved in it may have been harder for the King to bear than even the rejection of his general military demands. Anyhow there seems no doubt that upon learning the decision of the House in the matter of the army William did seriously contemplate retirement to Holland, after abdicating in favour of the Princess Anne, and that nothing but the firmness of Somers prevented him from carrying his resolution into effect. So at least Somers himself believed; and Somers's knowledge of the royal mind, as well as of the royal character, was distinctly superior

to that of Burnet, who treated the threat of withdrawal
as not seriously meant. And when, having schooled
himself to submit with dignity and grace to this rebuff,
he found himself churlishly denied the slight personal
favour which he subsequently requested, his bitterness
of feeling was, we may well believe, extreme.[1] The
whole incident is one which no Englishman of the
present day, whatever his politics, can look back upon
without a sense of shame.

William, it may be imagined, was not sorry to put an
end to a parliamentary session so fraught with unpleas-
ant incidents. Nor, after the settlement of the military
question, was there much more business to be done.
Its despatch, however, was attended by one occurrence
which deserves notice here as having prepared the way
for one of the gravest political conflicts of the reign.
Defeated by the manœuvre above referred to in their
attack upon the Crown grants, the country party brought
their forces to bear upon a position at once more limited
and more assailable. They demanded a commission of
inquiry into the disposal of the Irish forfeitures, and to
insure the accomplishment of their object they resorted
to the questionable expedient of "tacking" to a money
Bill which they were sending to the Upper House a
clause authorising the appointment of seven commissioners to carry out the proposed investigation. To this
virtual "ouster" of their jurisdiction over the question

---

[1] He writes in a letter to Lord Galway, Jan. 27, 1699: "It is
not possible to be more sensibly touched than I am at my not being
able to do more for the poor refugee officers who have served me with
so much zeal and fidelity. I am afraid the good God will punish the
ingratitude of this nation. Assuredly on all sides my patience is put
to the trial."

the Lords very naturally objected. They could not reject the Land Tax Bill, the measure to which this clause had been tacked, without creating national confusion; and rejection without amendment was their only constitutional alternative to accepting it—commissioners' clause, and all. They demurred, but ultimately yielded, under protest; and William, not as it seems without foreboding of future trouble, assented to the Bill with its irrelevant rider.

It was now the month of May, and the Houses, having held uninterrupted session ever since the 1st of January, had fairly earned their recess. On the 4th of the month the King came down to Westminster and bade his Parliament a cold adieu.

CHAPTER XIV

1699-1700

Death of the Electoral Prince of Bavaria—Renewed negotiations—
Second Partition Treaty—The Irish forfeitures—The Resumption
Bill—Will and death of the King of Spain.

THE political event on which William had founded
hopes of re-opening the army question has been indirectly referred to in the last chapter. This event,
as has been said, was one which might reasonably have
been thought likely to dispose the English Parliament
to a more liberal view of the military necessities of the
country by bringing once more into prominence a
European danger which diplomacy had been hitherto
believed to have averted. In the early days of 1699
the Electoral Prince of Bavaria—the youthful heir-
designate of the Spanish monarchy—took his departure
from a troubled world whose confusions were to be formidably increased by his quitting it. The English
Parliament, as we have seen, refused to allow the
Prince's death to modify their policy. But William
could not afford to overlook it; for it, of course, re-
opened at once the whole question which had been
closed by the First Partition Treaty, and rendered it
necessary to nominate a new successor to the Spanish

kingdom and its possessions in the New World. Louis
XIV. was the first to move in the matter. He instructed
De Tallard to sound William as to a new Treaty, and,
after one or two candidates had been mentioned and
rejected, it was finally agreed between the French and
English sovereigns that the Archduke Charles, the son
of the Emperor Leopold, should be the future King of
Spain and the Indies, and that the Milanese, which had
been allotted to him under the First Treaty, should go
to Louis, by whom it was to be bartered for Lorraine.
The arrangement was complete in all respects except
that of having received the sanction of the Emperor by
the summer or early autumn of 1699; but the rumour
of it caused a violent outbreak of indignation in Spain.
The Marquis of Canales, Spanish Ambassador at the
English Court, was instructed to protest, which he did
in terms so insolently imperious that William, on being
informed at Loo of the language used by him, at once
directed that the Marquis's passports should be handed to
him, and at the same time recalled our own ambassador
at Madrid. By whose means the provisions of the new
Treaty were communicated to the Spanish Court and
people is not certainly known; but considering that one
of the parties to whom it had been submitted rejected
it (for the Emperor at the eleventh hour refused to sign),
and, moreover, that another party—the French king—
had never, in all probability, sincerely assented to it,
there is no need for much speculation on this point.
Leopold had known and obvious motives for disclos-
ing it to the unhappy Charles, and Louis is more
than suspected of having private motives for doing
so. But whichever of the two was the medium of

communication, Louis was indisputably the gainer. The news aroused a powerful anti-Austrian feeling in the minds of the Spanish people, of which the French King, who was far better served at the Court of Madrid than the Emperor, was not slow to take advantage. From the autumn of 1699 till the 1st of November 1700, when the few and miserable days of Charles II. came to an end, the agents of France worked persistently, and in the end successfully, to overcome the Austrian leanings of the dying monarch, and to convince him that on grounds of patriotism, no less than of legal and moral obligation, he was bound to devise his dominions to his lawful French heir, and away from the Prince to whom Louis had solemnly agreed with William that they should pass.

The final consummation of these intrigues, however, was still a year distant, and meanwhile an incident of extreme interest, and at the time of exceeding gravity, in English politics, has to be recorded. On the 19th of November Parliament met again, and in a mood which boded ill for the relations between the sovereign and the third estate of his realm. The session began with one of the numerous abortive attacks made upon Somers in the course of his distinguished career, and an equally unsuccessful attempt was made to procure the disgrace of that perpetual bugbear of the Tories, Bishop Burnet. But these were merely in the nature of preliminary skirmishes; it was not long before hostilities were opened upon William and his Ministers in a more serious way. It will be remembered that at the close of the last session the Commons tacked to the Land Tax Bill a clause appointing seven commissioners to inquire into

the Irish forfeitures, and that the Lords, after some
demur to the manner in which the proposal was being
forced upon them, passed the measure.   The report of
these commissioners, who had been pursuing their inquiries in Ireland during the recess, was now ready, and
early in the session it was presented to Parliament,
signed by four of the commissioners, the other three
dissenting.   Disfigured by many exaggerations and
some wilful misstatements, this important document
contained, nevertheless, an amount of discreditable truth
sufficient not only to excite considerable popular feeling
against William at the time, but to inflict some permanent injury on his historical reputation.

The four commissioners reported that all the lands
in the several counties in Ireland belonging to the forfeited persons amounted, as far as they could reckon, to
1,060,762 acres, worth £211,623 per annum, and com-
puted therefrom to be of the capital value of £2,685,138.
That some of these lands had been restored to the old
proprietors by virtue of the Articles of Limerick and
Galway, or by his Majesty's favour through reversal of
outlawries, and royal pardons obtained chiefly by gratifications to such persons as had abused his Majesty's
royal bounty and compassion; and that besides these
restitutions, which they thought to be corruptly procured,
there were seventy-six grants and "custodians" under the
Great Seal of Ireland, of which they made a recital—as, for
instance, to the Lord Romney, three grants now in being,
containing 49,517 acres; to the Earl of Albemarle, in two
grants, 106,633 acres in possession and reversion; to
William Bentinck, Esq., Lord Woodstock (Portland's
eldest son), 135,820 acres of land; to the Earl of Athlone

in two grants, 26,480 acres; to the Earl of Galway one
grant of 36,148 acres, etc. That the estates so mentioned did not indeed yield so much to the grantees as
they were valued at, because as most of them had abused
his Majesty on the real value of their estates, so their
agents had imposed upon them, and had either sold or
let the greatest part of these lands at an undervalue;
but that after all deductions and allowances there yet
remained £1,699,343 : 14s. which they laid before the
Commons as the gross value of the estates forfeited since
the 13th day of February 1689, and not restored. The
commissioners went on, in excess, as it should seem, of
their attributions,[1] to report that William had conferred
the forfeited Irish estates of the late King James, estimated at 95,649 acres, worth £25,998 a year, on his
mistress, the Countess of Orkney. Excluding this item,
however, the value of the restorations and royal grants
against which the commissioners reported amounted, it
will be seen, to close upon a million sterling.

It is very probable, indeed it may be said to be certain,
that the total value of these forfeitures was grossly
exaggerated by the commissioners; it is possible that
it was to some extent wilfully exaggerated for party purposes. The lands forfeited in Ireland during the Revolution may have been worth "nearer half a million sterling
than two millions and a half." It does not seem to me,

---

[1] It was justly contended by the dissentient commissioners that
these lands had passed to William by his father-in-law's abdication in
1688, and did not therefore come properly within the purview of an
inquiry limited to forfeitures occurring since February 13, 1689. The
majority of the commission insisted, however, paradoxically enough,
that James's Irish estates were only forfeited on, and by, his invasion
of Ireland in March of the latter year.

however, that this is a point of the importance which
Macaulay seems to attach to it. Even if it could be
shown that the proportion of the royal grants to the
total forfeitures was unduly magnified through an over-
estimate of the value of the former, I cannot see that it
would affect the merits of the case. The real gist of the
charge against William in respect of these grants—
assuming, that is to say, that he was justified in making
them at all without the sanction of Parliament—is to be
sought not in a comparison of the royal benefactions
with the amount of the property at his disposal, but
in an examination of their proportions *inter se*. Even
if it be shown that he distributed property of the
value not of a million sterling, but of only a fifth of that
sum, it remains equally true in either case, that more
than one-tenth of his bounty went to a single favourite
who had little or no public services to show for them,
and very nearly an eighth to a young man whose only
claim upon him was that of being an able and faithful
servant's eldest son. The grants to Albemarle and
Woodstock are impossible to defend, and the latter
almost impossible to explain. William had already
loaded Portland with benefits, and to the vast estates
he had bestowed upon him in England his eldest son
would, in the natural course of events, succeed. On
what ground, either of justice or even of sentiment, it
could have been thought well to enrich the expectant
heir of so much English landed property with 135,820
acres of forfeited Irish land is a mystery which
has never been satisfactorily explained. As to the
grant to Albemarle, it was of even worse example.
Woodstock was at least the son of a counsellor to whom

William owed much, and whom he might conceivably
have regarded himself as rewarding in the person of his
heir; but what had Keppel, a mere favourite, a young
courtier with no other recommendations but his youth,
his good looks, and his complaisance, a personality too
closely recalling that of a "minion" of Henri Trois, and
which in the Jacobite libels, not wisely to be thus
supplied with colourable pretexts for their calumnies,
was openly so described — what, one cannot but ask,
had Keppel done to deserve a grant of 106,633 acres of
the forfeited Irish land?   Compare these two largesses,
Woodstock's and Albemarle's, with those bestowed on
Lord Romney, an ex-Secretary of State, and one of the
leaders of the movement which brought William to
England; on Lord Athlone, the stout Dutch soldier
who, as General Ginkel, had given and taken many a
hard knock in his master's service; on Lord Galway,
that gallant Marquis de Ruvigny who had turned the
flank of the Irish on the bloody day of Aghrim.
Albemarle's, the smaller of the two, is more than twice
that of Romney, nearly thrice that of Galway, more
than four times that of Athlone.   It was impossible for
William to contend in the face of this evidence that he
had simply been using the forfeited lands of Irish rebels
to reward those public servants who had done most by
valour in the field, or wisdom in the council-chamber,
to establish firmly on the throne of England, the
Prince chosen by the nation; and that therefore he was
merely anticipating the national reward which would
have been conferred upon them, and virtually drawing
upon one national fund in relief of prospective charges
upon another.   He could not even contend, as we have

seen, that this was the *main* use to which he had put
the forfeitures; for though wisdom and valour had
come in for a share of the spoils, their share was
lamentably smaller than that which was won by mere
arts of courtiership. There is, in short, no denying the
fact that while William applied a part of this property
to strictly public objects, or, in other words, to objects
to which, but for such application of it, the public would
have to contribute in another shape, he devoted far too
large a portion of it to purposes of purely private
benefaction, for which he would otherwise have had to
resort to drafts upon his Civil List.[1]

But even this does not exhaust all the disagreeable
elements in the transaction. Had the Irish forfeitures
been simply in the nature of property "within the
order and disposition" of the sovereign, and impressed
with only a constructive trust for the benefit of the
nation, the King's dealings with it would have been
open to grave reprehension. As a matter of fact, how-

[1] The grants to Lady Orkney, of which so much was made by the
country party at the time, raised a totally different question on another
level, so to speak, of political morality. These grants were made out
of William's inheritance from his predecessor; and though Macaulay
is no doubt abstractedly right in arguing that William should have
pensioned his mistress out of economies effected in his Civil List than
by alienating his hereditary revenue, the remark is from the practical
point of view somewhat of an anachronism. In our day, when the lands
of the Crown are formally vested in commissioners by the sovereign in
consideration of his Civil List at the commencement of each reign, the
quasi-national character of this property is fixed and emphasised.
But no sovereign before William's time had regarded it in this light,
or recognised any implied restraint upon alienation; and William,
with Charles II.'s grants to his numerous mistresses before his eyes,
may well be excused for thinking his gift to Lady Orkney not only
justifiable but laudably moderate.

ever, the property in question was the subject not of a
mere constructive trust, but of an express recognition on
William's part of its fiduciary character, and of a distinct
promise that Parliament, as representing the *cestui que
trust*, should have an opportunity of deciding on the
proper mode of its application.   On the 5th of January
1691 the King had closed the short autumn with
a speech, in which he assured the Houses that he would
not "make any grant of the forfeited lands in England
and Ireland till there be another opportunity of settling
that matter in Parliament, in such manner as shall be
thought most expedient."   This undertaking had reference to a Bill which had actually passed the Commons
for applying the Irish forfeitures, and which only failed
to become law because William, who was due at the
Congress then about to meet at the Hague, was compelled to prorogue Parliament before the Lords had had
time to consider the measure.   It is vain to contend
that this promise was fulfilled, because several " opportunities " were given to Parliament to deal with the
question—in the sense that several sessions were allowed
to pass without Parliament moving in the matter—
before William himself proceeded to grant away the
forfeited lands.   William was not entitled, under the
circumstances, to infer any surrender of parliamentary
control over the forfeitures from mere parliamentary
inaction.   Such an inference would in any case have
been a somewhat questionable one ; but this was a case
in which the wishes of one branch of the Legislature
had already been recorded in the form of a distinct
legislative project.   The King knew, in short, that the
Commons desired to make Irish rebellion as far as

possible pay for its own suppression; he knew that they looked to the value of the rebels' lands to afford partial relief to the English tax-payer from the heavy imposts to which he was being subjected; and when, knowing this, he proceeded to grant away large tracts of these lands, thus affected to the national service, at his own will and pleasure, and in many cases to persons whom the nation would never have consented to endow so munificently out of its own pocket, he was unquestionably dealing with his Parliament and people after a fashion which, in the case of a private individual standing in analogous relation to other parties, would be severely condemned. If he intended to ignore his promise of January 1691 altogether, his grants were mere high-handed usurpations of right; if he relied upon the mere "allowance of opportunities" in the manner above mentioned as being a fulfilment of that promise, then he was guilty of something which can only be described in modern phraseology as sharp practice.

Undoubtedly the House of Commons might have proceeded with more moderation than they displayed, but the majority in that House felt that they had a good, and what was still better, a popular case against the King and his advisers; they knew that the country was sore with the weight of taxation, and jealous of the amount of royal favour bestowed upon foreigners; and they felt that they might rely upon the combined force of these two sentiments to support them in extreme measures. Having gained their first triumph in the committal to the Tower of Sir Richard Levinge, one of the dissentient commissioners who had charged his colleagues with speaking disrespectfully of the sovereign in connection with these benefactions, they introduced the famous Resumption Bill, a measure by which all the royal grants were invalidated, and the whole of the alienated property resumed to the use of the State. In the Bill sent up to the Lords from the Lower House in 1690 it had been proposed to reserve a third part of the forfeitures to the King, and William was not without hopes that this reservation, which would just about have covered his grants to Woodstock, Albemarle, and the three other peers whose names have been mentioned above, would be renewed. The imperious majority, however, refused to hear of any such modification of their demands. They rejected a clause moved by Ministers for reserving at least some portion of the forfeitures to the King ; and they carried resolutions to the effect that "the advising, procuring, and passing of the grants in Ireland had been the occasion of contracting great debts, and laying heavy burdens upon the people ; that the said grants reflected highly upon the King's honour; and that the officers and instruments concerned in procuring and passing them had highly failed in the performance of their duty." These resolutions were presented to William at Kensington by the Speaker and leaders of the Opposition. William replied that he had thought himself bound to reward out of the forfeited property those who had served him well, and especially those who had borne a principal part in the reduction of Ireland. The war, he said, had undoubtedly left behind it a heavy debt, and he should be glad to see that debt reduced by just and effectual means.

The answer, though undoubtedly weak enough, seems scarcely open to one of the criticisms which

Macaulay pronounces upon it.[1] It would have been not
so much injudicious as absurd on William's part to
"hint" that the Irish forfeitures "could not justly be
applied to the discharge of the public debts." His
meaning could only have been that it would not be just
to the grantees to resume their property in order to
apply it to public uses. It would appear, however, that
the House of Commons understood his words in the
wider and less defensible sense. The Resumption Bill
was pushed vigorously through the House of Commons,
and in order to paralyze the expected resistance of the
Lords, the expedient of tacking was again resorted to.
The Bill was tacked to a Land Tax Bill for raising two
shillings in the pound for the service of the next year, and
then sent to the Upper House. It passed its second reading by a considerable majority, but in committee and on
the third reading several amendments were carried. It
is highly significant, however, that though William was
known to be very solicitous to obtain the confirmation
of at least some of his Irish grants, and though the
majority in the Lords in favour of the amendment may
be supposed desirous of doing all that they reasonably
could to gratify him, the Bill as regards his dealings with

---

[1] The context of the passage, "The Commons murmured, etc., 'His
Majesty tells us,' they said, 'that the debts fall to us, and the
forfeitures to him'" (*Hist. Eng.* v. 271), appears clearly to show that
Macaulay supposed William to be speaking of the whole of the
forfeitures as not justly applicable to the public debt. His own
previous words will just admit (though not in strict grammar) of the
construction that the King was referring only to the "one-fifth part
of these estates" which had passed to deserving grantees; but if this
is to be its construction, Macaulay's favourite boast that he had
written no sentence capable of being misunderstood would have to be
abandoned.

the Irish forfeitures was left untouched. The majority contented themselves with modifying certain arbitrary and inequitable provisions whereby the Lower House had sought to usurp jurisdiction over property which had never come to the Crown by forfeiture at all, and to grant estates and sums of money of their own authority, and without the constitutional intermediation of the Crown, to certain favoured individuals. Thus amended, the Bill was sent back to the Lower House, where it met of course with the very reception which the expedient of tacking was designed, in the event of its coming back with amendments, to secure for it. Parties had been much divided as to the policy of tacking the Resumption Bill to a money Bill; but as to the duty of resisting an attempt on the part of the Lords to amend a Bill sent up to them in this fashion parties were united. The amendments were rejected *nemine dissentiente*, and at the conference which followed the Lords were informed by the managers of the Commons that the point of constitutional practice was too well settled to be arguable, and that the Bill was left in their hands along with the responsibility of all the serious consequences which must follow its rejection. The Lords nevertheless for a time stood firm; they resolved by a majority of thirteen to adhere to their amendments, and on the following day the Bill was, on a second conference, returned once more to the Commons, by whom it was once more sent back to the Lords, with an intimation that the determination of the Lower House was unalterable. This was on the 10th of May, and the whole of that day and night the greatest public excitement prevailed. The deadlock between the two Houses had reached such a point that

if both refused to give way, and the supplies were
consequently lost, a complete dislocation of the
national business, accompanied in all probability by
dangerous popular disturbance, would have assuredly
followed.

From this peril the country was saved at the critical
moment by the good sense and magnanimity of William.
His behaviour was the more creditable to him because
not only was he eager, as has been said, for the rejection
of the Resumption Bill, but he had taken so active a
part in the attempt to bring about that result that surrender must necessarily subject him to additional humiliation. There can be no doubt from the account given
by Burnet, whose own painful perplexity between the
claims of courtiership and patriotism increases the value
of his testimony on the subject, that William had tried
hard to procure the defeat of the measure. "The King,"
says the Bishop, "seemed resolved to venture on all the
ill consequences that might follow the losing this Bill,
though these would probably have been fatal. As far
as we can judge either another session of that Parliament
or a new one would have banished the favourites and
begun the Bill anew with the addition of obliging the
grantees to refund all the mesne profits. Many in the
Lords, that in all other things were very firm to the King,
were for passing the Bill, notwithstanding the King's
earnestness for it, since they apprehended the ill consequences that were like to follow if it was lost." On the
5th of April he told Portland that if the Bill was not
stopped in the Upper House he should count all lost ; and
on the same day he declared that he was resolved not to
pass the Bill, and that the only question was whether he

should prorogue the Parliament on that day or on the following Monday. On or before the 10th of April he had reflected more maturely on the situation, and with that intuitive recognition of when to give way, which only strong rulers ever seem to exhibit, and which the masterful Elizabeth had displayed before him, he saw that the time had arrived to yield. He took steps to have it conveyed to his adherents in the Upper House that he desired the Bill to pass ; and on the sitting of the following day, May 11, the Lords withdrew their amendments and accepted the Bill in its original form. Thus passed away a most perilous crisis, and William, by the fine temper and moral courage with which he thus submitted to perhaps the most galling rebuke ever inflicted upon a monarch by a legislative assembly, must be admitted to have gone far to atone for the serious error of his previous action. He was, however, and not unnaturally, of opinion that he had done enough in the cause of the peace, and the next day, in order to prevent the presentation to him of an address from the Commons, praying that no person not a native, except Prince George of Denmark, should be admitted to his Majesty's Councils in England or Ireland, he came down and prorogued Parliament without a speech.

The whole of the year 1700 was destined to abound in fresh troubles for this sorely-tried and now fast waning life. No sooner had the English Parliament separated than the Scotch Parliament met ; and their first business was to espouse the cause of their foolish and unlucky countrymen who had taken part in the famous " Darien expedition," and were now under detention by the Spanish Government at Carthagena. The notable scheme in which these men had thus lost their liberty, and so many thousands of other Scotchmen their property, was originated by an adventurer of the name of Paterson, and depended for its success on the double assumption that the territorial owners of the country on which they proposed to found a trading station for the avowed purpose of diverting trade from these owners' hands into their own would respect their occupancy, and that the burning heat and malarious climate of an equatorial region would spare their lives. Neither of these assumptions had been realised. The sun and the swamps had thinned the number of the settlers to a handful, and this remnant had been besieged, forced to capitulate, and expelled from the isthmus by the forces of Spain. William promised, in reply to an address from the Edinburgh legislators, to demand the release of the Carthagena prisoners; but when the Scotch Parliament proceeded to pass a resolution affirming that the colony in Darien was a legal and rightful settlement, and that the Parliament would maintain and support the same, the King thought it high time to put a check on their proceedings. This he endeavoured to do through the royal commissioner by means of repeated adjournments carried to such an extent as to cause riots in Edinburgh, and at last, by dint of conciliatory replies to their resolutions, and possibly by gratifications of a more substantial kind, succeeded not only in pacifying his northern subjects on this matter, but in bringing them, before the close of the session at the end of the year, into a state of such loyal complaisance that, unlike their English brethren, the Scotch legislators voted for keeping on foot the whole of the land forces that existed in the kingdom when the session began.

The time was now fast approaching when William's military policy was to be justified by events. Throughout the whole of this year the struggle of rival Powers over the fast decaying body of the unhappy Charles had gone spiritedly forward at the Court of Madrid. The combatants, however, were unequally matched. On the side of France were enlisted the services of Cardinal Portocarrero, who soon succeeded in removing the King's confessor—an Austrian instrument—and substituting another in the French interests. The terrors of religion were then brought to bear upon the wretched sovereign in a strength sufficient to overcome his natural leanings in the matter of the disposition of his crown and kingdom towards his own Austrian flesh and blood. They persuaded the unhappy imbecile that he had been bewitched through Austrian agency; they persuaded the populace of Madrid that the partisans of Austria had brought about a famine. Having at last succeeded in utterly discrediting the rival party, and working upon the superstition of Charles until he believed that if he ousted his Bourbon heir from the succession he would be inevitably damned, the French faction finally induced him to sign a will appointing Philip, Duke of Anjou, universal successor to the Spanish monarchy. A month afterwards this miserable slave of the priest and the plotter at last obtained his manumission. He died on the 1st of November 1700, and William then learnt for the first time that the months of laborious negotiations spent on the successive framing of two carefully-drawn treaties had been completely thrown away. For a brief space of time, indeed, he remained in doubt whether Louis really intended to play him false, but before the middle of the month of November all uncertainty was at an end. Louis threw over the Partition Treaty and adopted the will. The Duke of Anjou was despatched into Spain with the historic exclamation touching the effacement of the Pyrenees—mountains certainly not in this instance removed by "faith,"—and William had the intolerable chagrin of discovering not only that he had been befooled, but that his English subjects had no sympathy with him or animosity against the royal swindler who had tricked him. "The blindness of the people here," he writes sadly to the Pensionary Heinsius, "is incredible. For though the affair is not public, yet it was no sooner said that the King of Spain's will was in favour of the Duke of Anjou, than it was the general opinion that it was better for England that France should accept the will than fulfil the Treaty of Partition."

CHAPTER XV

English indifference on the Spanish question—Death of James II. and Louis's recognition of the Pretender—Reaction in England—Dissolution of Parliament—Support of William's policy by its successor—The Treaties—Accident to William—His illness and death —Character—The Whig legend examined—His great qualities as man and ruler—Our debt to him.

THE insensibility of Englishmen to a danger which weighed heavily on the mind of William was exactly matched by his own indifference to one which appeared extremely serious to them. William dreaded the idea of a Bourbon reigning at Madrid, but he saw no very grave objection, as the two treaties showed, to Naples and Sicily passing into French hands. With his English subjects the exact converse was the case. They strongly deprecated the assignment of the Mediterranean possessions of the Spaniard to the Dauphin; but they were undisturbed by the sight of the Duke of Anjou seating himself on the Spanish throne. It has been said that on their own principles they ought to have disliked the will even more than the Partition Treaties, because the former document, in devising *all* the possessions of Spain to the Duke of Anjou, "gave precisely the same advantages to France on the Mediterranean" as she would

have obtained under the Treaties. But this argument
obviously begs the whole question against the English
view by assigning to the word "France" a meaning which
it was of the essence of that view to repudiate. The
very gist of the English case was that "France" and
"the second son of the French Dauphin barred from
the succession to the French Crown" were not con-
vertible terms. Had Englishmen in general so regarded
them, they would perhaps have been as jealous of the
Duke of Anjou's succession to the Spanish throne as was
William himself. They held, however,—whether rightly
or wrongly, and I have already stated my reason for
thinking that at the time and in the circumstances they
were wrong—that the elevation of Louis's grandson to
the Spanish throne did not mean the "solidarity" of
France and Spain.[1] But while the Duke of Anjou, considered as the owner of the two Sicilies, did not in their
opinion stand for "France," the Dauphin, who was to
have had them under the Partition Treaties, undeniably
did. The heir to the Crown of France of course *is*
France, not as a matter of opinion, but as a matter of
fact. The English view therefore, however mistaken on
the point of policy, was unassailable on the ground of
logic ; and its inherent plausibility, in addition to the
national dissatisfaction with the manner in which the
Treaties had been negotiated, would, in all probability,
have made it impossible for William to carry the
country with him in a war policy directed against
France.

But just as, under a discharge from an electric battery,

---

[1] That Louis intended it to mean this is pretty obvious from his
remark about the effacement of the Pyrenees.

two repugnant chemical compounds will sometimes rush into sudden combination, so at this juncture the King and the nation were instantaneously united by the shock of a gross affront. The hand that liberated the uniting fluid was that of the Christian king. On the 16th of September 1701 James II. breathed his last at St. Germains, and, obedient to one of those impulses, half-chivalrous, half-arrogant, which so often determined his policy, Louis XIV. declared his recognition of the Prince of Wales as *de jure* King of England. No more timely and effective assistance to the policy of its *de facto* king could possibly have been rendered. Its effect upon English public opinion was instantaneous; and when William returned from Holland on the 4th of November, he found the country in the temper in which he could most have wished it to be. Still he hesitated for a while as to whether or not he should dissolve Parliament. Sunderland, for whose astuteness and profound knowledge of English politics William entertained a respect unqualified, as was usual with that cool and cynical observer of men, by any repugnance he might have felt for the ex-Minister's political profligacy, had been consulted by him on this point through Somers both before and since the death of James; and this sagacious counsellor had urgently recommended a dissolution, predicting that it would result in a signal triumph of the Whigs. On the 7th of November William laid the question before his Privy Council, who were divided in opinion, and, acting on his own judgment, he then determined to dissolve. On the 11th of the month the royal proclamation to that effect was issued, and the new Parliament summoned to meet on the 31st of December. The result did not, indeed, completely bear out Sunderland's prediction, but it proved that a marked change had taken place in the opinion of the country; for, though the Tories managed still to hold their own in the smaller boroughs, the Whigs carried most of the counties and great towns. Their opponents, however, were strong enough to re-elect Harley to the Speakership, his nomination being seconded by his afterwards yet more famous political ally, Henry St. John, the future Lord Bolingbroke. William addressed the Houses in a speech of unusual length and earnestness, in which he recalled the "high indignity" offered to himself and the nation by Louis's recognition of the pretended Prince of Wales as King of England, and the dangers with which England and Europe were threatened by the elevation of his grandson to the Spanish throne. To obviate these dangers he had, he told them, concluded several alliances, and treaties for the conclusion of others were still pending. He went on to remind them that the eyes of all Europe were upon this Parliament, and "all matters at a standstill until their resolution was known. Therefore," said he, "no time ought to be lost; you have an opportunity, by God's blessing, to secure to you and your posterity the quiet enjoyment of your religion and liberties, if you are not wanting to yourselves, but will exert the ancient vigour of the English nation; but I tell you plainly my opinion is, if you do not lay hold on this occasion you have no reason to hope for another." He concluded with an exhortation, almost passionate for him, to lay aside "the unhappy fatal animosities" which divided and weakened them. "Let me conjure you to disappoint the only hopes of our enemies by your unanimity. I have shown, and will always show, how desirous I am to be the common father of my people; do you in like manner lay aside parties and divisions; let there be no other distinction heard of among us in future but of those who are for the Protestant religion and the present Establishment, and of those who mean a Popish prince and a French Government."

This stirring speech produced its due effect. Opposition in Parliament—in the country it was already inaudible—was completely silenced. The two Houses sent up addresses assuring the King of their firm resolve to defend the succession against the pretended Prince of Wales and all other pretenders whatsoever. The Commons declared independently—in those days addresses from the two Houses were not as now identical in terms —that they would to the utmost of their power enable his Majesty to make good all such alliances as he had made—an omission from the address of the Upper House which their Lordships subsequently supplied. Nor did the goodwill of Parliament expend itself in words. The Commons accepted without a word of protest the four treaties constituting the new Grand Alliance, though the inequality of some of their conditions as regarded England, and the self-seeking motives which actuated one at least of their continental signatories, were apparent on the face of them. The votes of supply were passed unanimously, and ere the Parliament had well completed the first fortnight of its existence a Bill of Attainder against the Prince of Wales—in which the Lords endeavoured, but in vain, to include Mary of Modena—had passed both Houses. But the King's

assent to this, as also to an Abjuration Bill directed to
the same object, had to be given by commission; for
William was now already sickening to his death. His
always feeble health had become feebler during the
winter; his constant asthma had told heavily upon
the condition of his lungs; his legs had swollen to an
extent which led his doctors, though erroneously it
would seem, to suspect dropsy; he had, in fact, arrived
at that state of body in which any accident might be
fatal. On Saturday, the 21st of February, he set out from
Kensington on horseback to hunt, according to his
weekly custom, at Hampton Court. On the road his
horse stumbled over a molehill,[1] and fell with his rider,
who fractured his right collar-bone. William was taken
to Hampton Court, where the bone was set, and the
surgeon, finding him feverish, recommended bleeding.
This he declined, and, contrary to advice, insisted on
returning that evening to Kensington, where it appeared that the setting of the bone had been displaced
by the motion of the carriage, and the operation had to
be repeated. William slept well, and for a few days no
signs of mischief appeared. But, as was afterwards
shown by the autopsy, the fall from his horse had
violently detached a diseased portion of his lungs from
its adhesion to the walls of the thoracic cavity, and this
had set up pulmonary inflammation. On the 28th of
February he found himself unable to attend Parliament
in person, and accordingly conveyed to the Houses by
way of message his last recommendation of a project

---

[1] The nature of the impediment lives for history in the Jacobite
toast which so grimly reflects the brutal passions of the time—"To
the little gentleman in black velvet that works underground."

which, ever since the beginning of his reign, he had had
much at heart—that, namely, of effecting a legislative
union between England and Scotland. On the next
day alarming symptoms appeared. The assent to the
Prince of Wales's Attainder Bill was given by commission, and a week later, on the 7th of March, when it became necessary to issue another commission for a similar
purpose, William was past the power of subscribing the
sign-manual, which had to be affixed by a stamp. "*Je
tire vers ma fin*," he murmured to Albemarle, who had
arrived from Holland the same night; and, as the per-
versity of fate had willed it, he who had from boyhood
sought death everywhere, had not for years perhaps
been so little prepared to meet it. "Sometimes he
would have been glad, he told Portland, to have
been delivered out of all his troubles, but he confessed
now he saw another scene, and could wish to live a little
longer." It was another scene indeed—the whole web
of his Spanish policy unravelled, his great enemy once
more powerful for mischief, the whole work of his life to
do again!

He lived through the night, but that was all. Burnet
and Tillotson had gone to him that morning and did not
quit him till he died. The Archbishop prayed with him
some time, but he was then so weak that he could
scarcely articulate. "About five o'clock on Saturday
morning he desired the Sacrament, and went through
the office with great appearance of seriousness, but could
not express himself; when this was done he called for
the Earl of Albemarle and gave him a charge to take
care of his papers. He thanked M. Auverquerque for
his long and faithful services. He took leave of the

Duke of Ormond, and called for the Earl of Portland, but before he came his voice quite failed; so he took him by the hand and carried it to his heart with great tenderness. Between seven and eight o'clock the rattle began; the commendatory prayer was said for him, and as it ended he died."

More than one hundred and eighty years have passed since that morning; but though the fierce political controversies which raged around the person and character of the dead man, leaving, perhaps, no quality but his courage unassailed, have long since subsided, some into utter silence, others into moderation, it is impossible to say that their disturbing force is altogether spent. A faint echo from those furious clamours may still be heard mingling with the voice of History; a ripple from those distant billows still breaks the mirror of her judgment. It could hardly be otherwise. The principles of which William was in part the voluntary and in part the unchoosing champion have triumphed so completely that they find nowadays no avowed opponent, and scarcely even any secret enemy; but it was William's destiny to have been identified in the promotion and defence of them with an English political party whose many excellent qualities as statesmen and citizens have been always associated with a moral and intellectual temper which, for a century and a half, has offered a standing provocation to men of every other political school. Fate made William of Orange a Whig hero, and in arranging his preliminary condition ordained also by inevitable sequence his exposure to some measure of the polemical resentments which his votaries have never failed to concentrate upon themselves. That the Whigs of his own day should have behaved as they did, on many occasions exceedingly ill to him, is no more unnatural than that they should have unduly exaggerated his virtues after his death. Both their ill-treatment and their excessive eulogy of him were, in different ways, the expression of the same modest confidence in their own civil deserts. The Whigs believed themselves entitled not only to an exclusive interest in a living Whig-made king, but also to as much capital as could be made out of his posthumous renown. If they behaved ill to him at times during his life, it was to assert the just claims of the Whig party; if they over-praised him when dead, it was by way of just tribute to the Whig virtues.

Far be it from me to suggest that William of Orange needs any such artificial additions to his legitimate glory. They are mentioned merely to account for and excuse the fact that an impartial review of his career and character needs to be commenced with what might otherwise seem words of captious disparagement. It is absolutely necessary to strip off the draperies of partisanship in order to see the real man beneath; but that truly heroic figure can well afford it.

William of Orange, I maintain then, is not to be regarded as altogether that " patriot king," that " sovereign of the people," which it has pleased his Whig devotees to discover in him, still less as that sort of anticipatory and prophetic political philosopher for which he passes in the legend of some Whig constitutionalists. No doubt he had a distinct popular fibre in his nature. The great-grandson of his great-grandfather can hardly have been wanting in sympathy with popular aspirations, or in belief in the might and virtue of

popular forces. But such sentiments have been the
birthright of many a man whose instincts were the
very reverse of democratic; and there is no reason to
think that William either foresaw or would have
relished that growth of the democratic element in
English government to which he inevitably contributed
so powerful a stimulus. He was not, it must be remembered, a democrat even in his own country; on the
contrary, his strongest impulses were essentially of aristo-
cratic origin. It was not his Protestant enthusiasm,
though this was ardent enough, nor his love of his
country and his hatred of foreign dictation, though
these passions were strong and sincere enough, which
were the dominant influences in moulding his youthful
character. It was pride of ancestry, the memory of
William the Silent, resentment at the fallen fortunes of
his house, and resolution to restore them. These it was
which first inspired him with an ambition essentially
personal in its character, and it was not till this ambition had been gratified by his elevation to higher digni-
ties even than his forefathers, that the other impulses of
birth or training can be said to have begun to sway
him at all. And until that ambition was gratified he
was not only capable of all the virtues of the ambitious,
but an adept in their vices also. He was but sixteen
when he taught his mother the wisdom of disarming
the suspicion of the Pensionary De Witt by pretended
cordiality, and earned the criticism of the shrewd
French envoy d'Estrades that he was "a great dissem-
bler, and omitted nothing to gain his ends." So, too,
one can hardly doubt that it was ambition rather than
zeal for liberty and Protestantism that first inspired him

with that design of intervention in England, which must have just taken shape in his mind shortly after the return of Dykvelt from his mission of 1687. His succession, or rather his wife's succession, was safe enough if Mary of Modena bore no male issue to James. But she might and did bear such issue, in a child whose claims could only be set aside by a revolution; and even had no heir apparent been born to the throne, the position of William accepting the English crown conjointly with his wife in his capacity as liberator of the English people would be something very different from that of a king-consort, which was all he could otherwise have hoped to be. It is surely not unjust to a man of William's antecedents to believe that from the hour that he learned the strength of his party in England, down to the hour when he was presented with the crown in the banqueting chamber at Whitehall, he had eyes for little else than the great European future which would open before him as King of England; and that any hesitations he may have shown in accepting the sovereignty were as purely politic as those of Cæsar at the Lupercal.

As regards his attitude towards English political institutions in general, and the *voluntary* element in his share in developing them, the Whig legend appears to me more purely mythical still. At no time in his life did William show the slightest personal predilection for or even faith in parliamentary institutions, still less in party government. He looked upon the English Parliament as a clumsy and irritating instrument, blunt at one part, dangerously double-edged at another, which he was nevertheless bound to work with and make the

best of. That he was the first to try the system of
a party ministry and party government is, as I have
essayed to show, a fact of little significance. He tried
it as he tried other means of managing the apparently
otherwise unmanageable, as he had at first tried divid-
ing offices of State among the leading men of both
parties, and as he had tried and continued to try the
method of corruption for the rank and file. As to any
preference of one English party to another there is no
trace of such a feeling in his mind. From the moral
point of view, I imagine, he regarded most of the
leaders of both parties with an equal, and, it may be,
with an equally just, contempt; but with his intellectual
appreciations he never allowed his moral judgment to
interfere.   He used the unscrupulous Tory Marlborough and the unscrupulous Whig Sunderland with
an impartial indifference to their political profligacy.
He made trial, in fact, of all English public men and of
all political expedients to serve his European ends,
which were sometimes but not always English ends
also; and thus it was that though he experimentalised
with the strict party system in order to secure a Parliament which would support the war energetically in
1695, yet in the next Parliament, his immediate object
being gained, he showed no disposition to prosecute that
experiment on abstract political grounds. It is impossible to represent a ruler of this kind, however wise
and moderate, as *consciously* training our parliamentary
institutions upon the peculiar lines of growth which
they subsequently followed.

Yet after all these deductions there remains to
William, both as a European statesman and as a bene-

factor to our country, an ample margin of renown. Of his moral and mental stature as a man it is scarcely necessary to speak. It must be patent to all but the dullest prejudices of our day as it was to all but the fiercest passions of his own. It is the highest praise of his high qualities to say that our impression of them easily survives the reaction from idolatry, and that after we have thrown aside the magnifying-glass of Whiggism the objects which it was used to exaggerate still fill the eye. If William had not all the virtues which belong to the patriot and philosopher, he had all that go to the making of the hero. Even Macaulay, who has over painted both his king-craft and his statesmanship, has not laid on the colours of his heroism with too bold a hand. Sagacious as he undoubtedly was in counsel, dexterous as he was in the management of men, keen as was his outlook on European politics, and resourceful as he was in meeting its exigencies, it is possible to contend that his Whig eulogist has credited him with far more than the keenness and sagacity, the dexterity and resource, which he possessed. But such eulogy does not, for it could not, materially exaggerate his great features as a man—his patience of delay and disappointment, his fortitude under disaster, his imperturbable composure in moments of crisis, his lofty magnanimity, which from its high place seemed literally to overlook rather than to forgive injuries, his haughty courage, which thought it equal shame to glance aside at the lurking assassin and to turn away from the open foe. His character was stern, forbidding, unamiable, contemptuously generous, as little fitted to attract love as it was assured of commanding respect ; but it bears in every lineament the unmistakable stamp of greatness. And his achievements were as great as his character. His record as a ruler pure and simple, as a mere expert in the art of governing, has never been surpassed, perhaps never equalled, in history. The showy administrative exploits of a Napoleon with vast armies at his back, and the pen of a despotism in his hand, appear to me to sink into insignificance when compared with those of this ruler of four nations—a constitutional sovereign in England and Scotland, the chief of a republic in Holland, and a military autocrat, governing by the sword alone, in Ireland,—who for eleven years successfully directed the affairs of these alien and often mutually hostile communities, and who throughout all that time held in one hand the threads of a vast network of European diplomacy, and in the other the sword which kept the most formidable of European monarchs at bay. Nor should we omit from the comparison that he did all this under moral restraints and physical disadvantages to which Napoleon was a total stranger, impeded by obligations to law, municipal and international, which Napoleon set cynically at defiance, and distressed throughout his life by bodily ailments which never troubled the Corsican's iron frame.

Nor in what has been written in criticism of the Whig legend would I for a moment be suspected of undervaluing the debt which Englishmen owe to William of Orange. It is not necessary to exalt him into a divinely inspired progenitor of the British Constitution in order to recognise fully the greatness of the services which he rendered to it. He was not "Father of the Constitution" in the sense in which the poet is the father of his poem, or the philosopher of his theory; but assuredly

he was so in the sense in which we say that a child
has found a "second father" in an upright guardian,
who, while not, it may be, comprehending his character,
or in sympathy with his spirit, or foreseeing his future,
has yet been his vigilant protector through the perils of
childhood, and has accounted for his patrimony to the
uttermost farthing.   That William stood in this relation
to our modern English polity throughout his too short
reign, and that he loyally discharged its obligations, is
indisputable.   The virtues which enabled him to do so
were mainly three, which are essential to all good and
faithful guardianship, whether of children or constitutions
—the virtues of good sense, self-restraint, and honesty.
And the greatest of these three is honesty.   William's
practical wisdom always told him the moment when to
yield in a struggle with his Parliament; and when that
moment arrived his naturally passionate temper never
failed to answer to the rein.   But even at those moments
there would often have been an evil alternative open to
him, from which the fundamental integrity of his nature
always turned aside.   He scrupled not to use all the arts
of political "management" which were sanctioned by the
lax morality of his day; he exerted his prerogative
freely to gain his ends; but he knew that the compact
between him and his people was that in the last resort
the will of the people should prevail, and this compact he
never attempted either to violate or to evade.   Here
he was as emphatically a *Rè Galantuomo*, a "King Honest-
man," as was Victor Emmanuel himself.

> "Hos ante effigies majorum pone tuorum,
> Præcedant ipsas illi, te consule, virgas."

Rulers who have earned this name may justly rank it,

if only for its rarity, above every other title of honour—
even though, themselves the creators or regenerators of
nations, they can look back upon the splendid achievements of the Counts of Nassau, or the long ancestral·
glories of the House of Savoy.

THE END

Printed by R. & R. CLARK, *Edinburgh*.

TWELVE ENGLISH STATESMEN.

* *A Series of Short Biographies, not designed to be a complete roll of famous Statesmen, but to present in historic order the lives and work of those leading actors in our affairs who by their direct influence have left an abiding mark on the policy, the institutions, and the position of Great Britain among States.*

OLIVER CROMWELL. By FREDERIC HARRISON.

TIMES :—" Gives a wonderfully vivid picture of events."

ST. JAMES'S GAZETTE :—" A model biography of its kind. . . . So much has been written on the subject, so carefully and critically has it been examined, that it seemed doubtful whether a writer attempting to treat of the hero of the epoch within the limits of an essay would not find himself overwhelmed by the mass of his material. Mr. Harrison, however, has steered clear of this danger. His work has unity and completeness. . . . He has proved once more that style, taken in its broadest sense of lucidity of arrangement, unity of conception, and just proportion of treatment, is an essential quality of a good history."

WILLIAM III. By H. D. TRAILL.

SATURDAY REVIEW :—" He has devoted himself mainly, if not wholly, to his title-subject of William III. as an English statesman. . . . The various questions requiring treatment are handled throughout with a perfect absence of prejudice, and with that faculty of judging evidence which the historians of special periods and special persons in our day display perhaps less often than any other quality. . . . The general narrative is also good, and though Mr. Traill does not pretend to deal with military matters with any extreme minuteness, his handling of them is judicious and thorough. . . ."

WALPOLE. By JOHN MORLEY.

ST. JAMES'S GAZETTE :—" It deserves to be read, not only as the work of one of the most prominent politicians of the day, but for its intrinsic merits. It is a clever, thoughtful, and interesting biography."

WORLD :—" This admirable little book is in style, arrangement, and proportion the model of what history on such a scale should be."

SATURDAY REVIEW :—" A very interesting and excellent book. . . . Mr. Morley has written as good a book as, for the honour of letters, we could have wished him to write."

CHATHAM. By JOHN MORLEY.

PITT. By LORD ROSEBERY.

TIMES :—" There are abundant proofs in this brilliant and fascinating little book that Lord Rosebery possesses literary gifts of a very high order. . . . The style is terse, masculine, nervous, articulate, and clear ; the grasp of circumstance and character is firm, penetrating, luminous, and unprejudiced ; the judgment is broad, generous, humane, and scrupulously candid, even when it provokes dissent ; and the whole book is irradiated with incessant flashes of genial and kindly humour, with frequent felicities of epigrammatic expression. . . . It is not only a luminous estimate of Pitt's character and policy, at once candid, sympathetic, and kindly ; it is also a brilliant gallery of portraits set in a background of broadly-sketched political landscape. The portrait of Fox, for example, is a masterpiece."

MORNING POST :—" None of the many biographical sketches published during recent years will better repay perusal than this, and certainly none has been marked on the whole by a more impartial judgment of history, whether national or individual."

DAILY NEWS :—" Requires no further recommendation than its own intrinsic merits. . . . It is in many respects, and those not the least essential, a model of what such a work should be. . . . By far the most powerful, because the most moderate and judicious defence of Pitt's whole career ever yet laid before the world."

PEEL. By J. R. THURSFIELD, M.A., late Fellow of Jesus College, Oxford.

DAILY NEWS :—" A model of what such a book should be. We can give it no higher praise than to say that it is worthy to rank with Mr. John Morley's *Walpole* in the same series."

MACMILLAN AND CO., LONDON. 10.12.91.

www.ingramcontent.com/pod-product-compliance
Lightning Source LLC
Chambersburg PA
CBHW020612030726
47497CB00007B/2212

* 9 7 8 3 3 3 7 4 2 3 7 2 8 *